"I'm Celie

The name hi_____d abruptly. This was Celie Donovan.

"Sorry you've come all this way for nothing," Matthew said, making little effort to conceal his disgust, "but Kiera isn't here. She's on her way to Mexico."

"Mexico? What's she doing in Mexico?"

As if you don't know, Matthew wanted to say. *As if you aren't Miss New York City's number one party girl, smelling like cigarette smoke and showing up on my doorstep in spike heels in the middle of the night.*

KIM O'BRIEN grew up in Bronxville, New York, with her family and many pets—fish, cats, dogs, gerbils, guinea pigs, parakeets, and even a big Thoroughbred horse named Pops. She worked for many years as a writer, editor, and speechwriter for IBM in New York. She holds a master's in fine arts in writing from Sarah Lawrence College in Bronxville, New York, and is active in the Fellowship of The Woodlands Church. She lives in The Woodlands, Texas, with her husband, two daughters, and, of course, pets.

Books by Kim O'Brien

HEARTSONG PRESENTS
HP641—The Pastor's Assignment
HP829—Leap of Faith

A Whole New Light

Kim O'Brien

Heartsong Presents

Many thanks to Kathleen Y'Barbo and Kelly Hake. Without the help of these two awesome Christian women and amazing writers, this book would never have happened.

A note from the Author:
I love to hear from my readers! You may correspond with me by writing:

Kim O'Brien
Author Relations
PO Box 721
Uhrichsville, OH 44683

ISBN 978-1-60260-500-8

A WHOLE NEW LIGHT

Our mission is to publish and distribute inspirational products offering exceptional value and biblical encouragement to the masses.

PRINTED IN THE U.S.A.

one

"You working late again, Celie?"

Celie Donovan lowered the nozzle of the portable steam presser and smiled at James Terelli who had escaped his office in accounting and was now standing behind her, clutching what was probably his sixth cup of coffee. "Libby wants all the outfits ready to ship Wednesday morning. You know she's going to go over everything with a magnifying glass."

At George Marcus Designs, perfect was the name of the game. A loose thread, a minuscule sag in the drapery, a hemline a fraction too long or short, elicited an immediate and scathing dressing-down from head designer Libby Ellman.

Celie didn't like the woman's managerial style but respected her flair for design. With Libby's help, George Marcus was one of the top design houses in New York City and arguably the world. "What are you still doing here, James?"

"Ah, show stuff, lots of invoices." James took a long swallow of coffee. "Besides, Frieda's cousin is visiting from Atlanta. Last night it was *Steel Magnolias*. Tonight it's *Beaches*. Why anyone wants to see a movie that makes them cry is beyond me."

Celie laughed and checked the hemline for the third time. "It's a girl thing, James. You need to embrace your feminine side." Judging from the way his hand shook, James also needed to embrace the idea of caffeine-free coffee. She'd been trying for more than a year to get James to cut back.

"I have enough exposure to my feminine side in this business." He gestured around the room. "I'm surrounded by dresses all day long."

"And you love it."

"Who wouldn't love the long hours, high stress, and low pay?" James pushed aside a bolt of chartreuse satin and perched on the edge of the worktable. "A bit of fatherly advice. Go home, Celie. Don't let Libby work you so hard that you don't have time to get your own outfits ready." He pointed the coffee cup at her. "This is your big chance, and you only get one in this business."

He didn't have to tell her this. Ever since she had been a little girl using a box of crayons to sketch, Celie had dreamed about being a designer. Growing up, she'd practically learned to read by poring over magazines like *Harper's Bazaar*, *Elle*, and *Glamour*.

"I know. Every time I think about it, I feel as green as"—she pointed to the bolt of fabric near James—"that satin."

It was true. Even now as she slipped a protective plastic covering over the tangerine silk, her stomach rolled as if she were on the Staten Island Ferry. The Fashion Walk of Fame was Saturday. What if she stunk? What if everyone hated her dresses?

Although Libby had approved her sketches and George Marcus had selected Celie out of everyone else at the store, she couldn't quiet her preshow nerves.

"Don't worry. You're going to be a hit." James nodded knowingly. "I may work in accounting, but I have spies everywhere."

"Just promise me you and Frieda will be there." She'd feel much better if James and his wife were at the show.

"You know we'll be there," James said. "So will the other design assistants, the administrative staff, and as many of the cleaning crew as we can slip in. We're all pulling for you, Celie."

"Thanks, James." Her throat went tight. "You know that means everything to me. I can't wait for you and Frieda to meet my parents. They're flying in the day after tomorrow."

The thought of her parents coming sent a pleasant shiver of expectation through her. They'd never been to Manhattan before, and she couldn't wait for them to see the Empire State Building, Broadway, Rockefeller Center, and of course, the Garment District.

"They've got to be proud of you, Celie. Having your dresses modeled in the Fashion Walk of Fame is a huge accomplishment for any designer, much less one as young as you are."

Celie felt herself blush. Her parents *were* proud of her. Her mother had mailed her a photo of the banner her parents had placed on the window of their dry cleaning business. It read: HOME OF FASHION WALK OF FAME DESIGNER CELIE DONOVAN. There had even been an article in the town paper.

"Thirty isn't that young," Celie joked.

"It is to me," James said. "You're barely out of diapers."

"Like you're so ancient. You're not even old enough to be vintage." Celie scanned the contents of a plastic bag to make sure all the accessories that went with the gown were there—the Jimmy Choo stilettos, the David Yurman gold spiral earrings and sterling-silver bracelet.

"Just don't go and forget the little people when you're rich and famous."

"I don't think that's going to be a problem." Celie smiled at the man who had been her friend ever since she'd found him frantically searching the showroom for a clean shirt and tie. He'd accidentally spilled coffee all over himself and had been just about to step into a meeting with George Marcus and the board of directors. There were no men's shirts in the store—all the company's designs were for women. Within minutes, Celie had transformed a woman's silk scarf into a stylish tie that coordinated perfectly with James's suit and completely covered the stain. He earned high praise not only for his professional presentation but also for his personal sense of style.

James crumpled the Styrofoam cup and tossed it in the trash can. "You ready to go? I don't like you taking such a late train."

"Just a few more minutes, James."

It took more than a few minutes. Celie ended up taking the 10:40 p.m. out of Grand Central Station. The train was nearly empty, and she had no trouble finding a seat. She closed her eyes as the train slid forward through the long black tunnel. Best to nap while she could. It might be her only sleep that night. She wanted to add a few beads to her strapless evening dress, and she still had more work to do on the hand-painted floral gown. James would kill her if he knew she'd taken that dress home, but what else was she supposed to do? Milah, a single mom and the new assistant designer, had accidentally damaged the dress when she'd tried to press it. Since Celie had been the one to paint the fabric in the first place, she had offered to fix it. Milah, fearing she'd be fired if anyone found out, had begged Celie to fix it secretly. It went against store policy to bring a dress home without permission, but Milah's tears had been impossible to ignore. Celie felt confident she could slip the dress back on the rack just in time for Libby's inspection in the morning.

It was raining lightly a little more than an hour later when she stepped off the train at the Stamford station. She pulled the thin trench coat around her a little more tightly. The flirty little skirt and cotton top had been optimistic choices, but she hadn't been able to resist the lightweight fabrics. Spring might have officially arrived, but the temperature refused to recognize it. She'd be surprised if it were even fifty degrees.

She walked briskly off the platform, her Jimmy Choo heels clicking on the concrete, and retrieved her Honda from the outdoor parking lot. Stamford was pretty much empty as she drove through the business district. People went home after work, unlike Manhattan.

She turned onto Hickory Hill Road. Halfway up she smelled smoke. Her heart began to thump, and she drove a little faster. She knew it wasn't someone barbecuing. The smell of smoke grew stronger as she reached the top of the hill. Three yellow road barriers blocked her from driving any farther down the street. She pulled the Honda to the side of the road and stepped into the cold, rainy night. Clutching her purse, she began to run. In the distance, she saw the flickering blue lights of a parked police car and beyond that three fire trucks. The smell of smoke was so strong now that she could taste its acrid bitterness.

A stab of fear propelled her forward. She pushed her way through the crowd that had gathered behind a line of yellow tape and police barriers. *Oh, God, no!* She stifled a cry at the sight of flames pouring out of the shattered windows of her apartment building. This couldn't be happening. She could feel the urge to scream rising up in her. Her fist clenched, and a low moan escaped her.

Firemen in bulky tan coats were everywhere—on the ground and in baskets at the top of ladders. They pointed gushing hoses at the building, drenching it in water that seemed powerless to extinguish a fire that sparked and crackled as if it enjoyed devouring the building. *Dear Lord, what happened? Had everyone gotten out all right?*

She scanned the faces in the crowd around her. "What happened? What's going on?" She spoke to anyone and everyone, but no one answered. Their shell-shocked, haggard faces seemed to look right through her. Behind the police barricade, she spotted a man wearing a dark jacket with Fire Marshal written across the front. She was about to try to climb over the wooden barrier when the man lifted a megaphone.

"Good evening, folks. My name is Edward Townser, and I'm the fire marshal. First of all, I'd like to say how sorry I am that this happened. If you have any information about how the fire may have started, I'd appreciate it if you would give me your statement." He paused as the crowd shuffled, but no one stepped forward. "Secondly, I am declaring this building a total loss. This means you will not be allowed inside the building for any reason. The Red Cross is getting set up at the other end of the parking lot. They will help you with food and clothing as well as provide shelter for those who need it."

"Did everyone get out okay?" Celie shouted. She felt sick at the thought of Mrs. Jacobs, who had recently had a hip replacement, stuck inside the burning building. The Krenzincos had young children. Were they okay?

"We're in the process of determining that right now," the fire marshal replied. "We'll let you know as soon as we hear anything."

Someone patted her shoulder. She turned. It was old Mr. Arnold from 304-B. She gave him a hug, and they clasped hands and prayed.

Her hair was soaked, and the night's chill seemed to have worked its way right into her bones before the fire marshal made the next announcement that there had been no fatalities. Celie whispered a prayer of thanks and walked over to the Red Cross station. She stopped when she saw the long line of people waiting for help.

The enormity of what had happened began to hit her. Her legs started to shake, and she leaned heavily against the side of a car for support. *The dresses! The hand-painted silk. The layered peach chiffon. The beaded black and gold gown!* She bit her lip hard. *All gone—and so is my career. I am so dead when Libby finds out what happened.*

Lord, she prayed, *what am I going to do?*

Her mind immediately began to spin. She could call James and get his advice. No. He would try to intervene on her behalf and get in trouble by association. She could drive back to Manhattan and start sewing. But even if she worked all night, she wouldn't be able to replace the ruined gowns.

It began to rain harder. Celie felt cold wetness trickle down the back of her bowed neck. *Call Kiera*, a voice inside seemed to say. *She'll know what to do.* Yes. She'd call Kiera, and together they'd figure a way out of this mess. Celie nearly dumped the contents of her handbag searching for her cell phone.

She finally found it and punched the speed dial. *Come on, Kiera, pick up.* The call rang into voice mail. Celie wanted to cry with disappointment. "Kiera," Celie said, "I really need you. Please call me. There was a fire." Celie's throat tightened, and she pressed her hand to her eyes to push back the tears.

"I'm not injured. But I'm in trouble. Just call me as soon as you can. Okay?" She flipped the phone shut and swiped her eyes again. Surely the fire was more important than their recent disagreement. Maybe Kiera had gone to bed early to get ready for an early morning fashion shoot. Yes, that had to be it.

I'll drive to her apartment. Her apartment buzzer is loud enough to wake the dead. And when she finds out what happened, she'll help me figure out what to do.

Her hands shook as she searched her purse for her keys. She'd almost reached her car when she remembered Kiera would be in Connecticut this week. She bit her lip, thinking hard. Kiera had said something about doing some catalog modeling. Celie couldn't remember the name of the company, but she did recall Kiera joking about having to stay at her family's apple orchard. "The house where time stands still," she'd said.

Celie stepped into the car just to get out of the rain. She could feel the panic creeping back, blocking her ability to think logically. What was the name of the town? *Something biblical*, she thought. *Bethlehem. That's right. Kiera mailed both our Christmas cards from the post office there so the stamp would say Bethlehem.* She searched her day timer and found an address but no phone number. It didn't matter. She'd find the orchard.

Celie started the Honda's engine, made a U-turn, and headed for I-95 North.

two

Toaster's barking awakened him. Swinging his legs over the side of the bed, Matthew Patrick reached for a pair of jeans and a sweatshirt. For the past several nights, there'd been a fox stalking the barn. It was after the pygmy goats.

He pulled back the curtain and strained to look through the rain-streaked glass. Nothing but darkness and the fog of his own breath. Good. The motion detectors hadn't triggered the lights at the barn. No fox.

Toaster continued to make urgent, high-pitched noises. The dog might bark soprano, but he had the heart of a lion. Something was wrong.

"Mom, you all right?" he called into the dark house.

"Yeah, but Toaster won't quiet. You think it's the fox again?"

"No." Matthew padded downstairs in his bare feet. Toaster charged ahead and began urgently barking at the front door. Matthew pulled back the edge of the curtain in the living room. Through the falling rain, he spotted a small four-door sedan of a dark color—maybe blue or gray—parked in their driveway. Just sitting there. No headlights. He couldn't tell if it was empty or not. He thought about retrieving his rifle and then stared some more at the unfamiliar car.

It was three o'clock in the morning. Whoever was sitting there and whatever he wanted, it wasn't good news. Good news did not arrive in the middle of the night and sit in the driveway on a rainy night that couldn't be warmer than forty degrees. He'd get the gun.

"What is it?" his mom called from her bedroom. Her voice rang with worry. "What's going on?"

"There's a car in the driveway, Mom," Matthew said. "Stay in your room and let me handle this."

12

"You think it's Kiera?"

"No. Please stay in your room."

Before he could get the gun, though, the car door opened and a small figure stepped into the rain. Hunched over, a small woman in a trench coat and a pair of high-heeled boots raced across his driveway. A moment later, she knocked at the front door.

Matthew flipped on the porch lights and cracked open the front door. She was young—Kiera's age—but far shorter than his sister. This woman barely reached his shoulder. She had pale skin, and her dark-colored hair hung shoulder-length in wet strands around her face.

"I'm sorry to bother you," the woman said. "I was going to wait until morning, but then the dog started barking. I saw the lights go on in the house." She peeked around him. "Is Kiera home? I'm one of her friends."

Matthew relaxed slightly. Now he understood the late arrival. She must have just heard. "I'm sorry, but Kiera's already gone. She left two days ago."

His mother's voice was sharp with fear. "Who's there? What's going on, Matthew?"

"A friend of Kiera's."

The next thing he knew, Toaster shot past his legs and ran onto the front porch, barking at the woman as if he might attack then messing up his tough-guy act by wagging his skinny little tail. "Get in here, Toaster."

As usual the dog paid no attention whatsoever to him. Toaster kept barking and circling. His mom'd kill him if the dog caught a cold. He opened the door wider and asked the woman to come inside. As he'd hoped, the dog followed. As the woman stood in the foyer, Toaster dropped the guard-dog act and began sniffing the woman's high-heeled boots with great interest.

The woman crouched and began petting Toaster. "Look how pretty you are," she said. "But what happened to your hair?"

Matthew almost laughed. Toaster did resemble the survivor of some scientific experiment that had gone terribly wrong.

"He's a Mexican Hairless. He's supposed to look all bald like that."

The woman smiled. "Well, he's cute. And he's got really sweet bangs."

Matthew found himself smiling back. "His name is Toaster, and I'm Matthew Patrick. Kiera's brother." He extended his hand. The woman's fingers were cold. Their slender bones felt incredibly delicate in his hands. He smelled a very faint trace of smoke on her.

"I'm Celie Donovan. Nice to meet you."

The name hit him as sharp as a slap. He released her hand abruptly. This was Celie Donovan?

"Sorry you've come all this way for nothing," Matthew said, making little effort to conceal his disgust, "but Kiera isn't here. She's on her way to Mexico."

"Mexico? What's she doing in Mexico?"

As if you don't know, Matthew wanted to say. *As if you aren't Miss New York City's number one party girl, smelling like cigarette smoke and showing up on my doorstep in spike heels in the middle of the night.*

"On a cruise," his mom answered. "Kiera is taking a vacation cruise to Cozumel."

He turned, and there his mother was, on the second floor landing, looming over the top of the staircase with only her walker standing between them and disaster. "Go back to bed, Mom. Kiera's *friend*"—he paused significantly so his mother would know this woman was the exact opposite—"was just leaving."

"Leaving?" His mother's voice rose. "Matthew Joseph Patrick, you are not letting one of Kiera's friends go out in weather like this. Have you lost your senses?"

"It's all right," Celie said. "I'm so sorry to have bothered you. Please ask Kiera to call me the next time you talk to her."

"You shouldn't be going anywhere tonight," his mom stated. "Matthew, please bring in this girl's luggage and show her to Kiera's room."

The last place Matthew wanted Celie to stay was in his sister's room. He didn't want this woman touching Kiera's things, sleeping in her bed. Not after what she'd done.

"Really, Mrs. Patrick," Celie protested. "It's okay. I love driving at night. There's less traffic, and the moon and stars are so pretty."

"There are no moon and stars out tonight. It's raining." His mother's voice brooked no argument. "The road's probably flooding. We'll talk more in the morning, but for now, you stay with us." She nodded at him as if he agreed with her, which he clearly didn't. "Matthew, take Celie's coat and go get her luggage."

He wanted to argue but not with his mother perched precariously at the top of the stairs. As Celie protested about not wanting to impose, etc., etc., he reached his arms out for the trench coat.

She untied the sash, unbuttoned the coat, and then it was in his hands. Matthew blinked.

That purple skirt hugged her shapely hips then ended with little flippy pleats just above her knees. And if that wasn't enough, there were the textured stockings for his eyes to contend with. Her black leather high-heeled boots rose to just above her ankles. The shirt, some sort of frothy white concoction, had more froufrou than he'd ever seen in his life. She was lovely, which at the moment wasn't something in her favor.

"I'll get your luggage."

"I don't have any," Celie admitted. She pushed a strand of chin-length hair behind her ear.

What in the world had happened to have her show up in the middle of a rainy night with no luggage? Matthew bit his tongue. Whatever it was, he didn't care. "I'll just show you to your room, then." With her coat still clutched in his hands, he led her up the stairs.

His mother stepped back to give them room, and as they passed, she had the nerve to wink at him. Even worse, she said to Celie, "What a lovely outfit."

"Thank you, Mrs. Patrick," Celie said. "And thank you so much for letting me stay the night. There was a fire, you see, at my apartment building, and. . ." Celie felt her throat get tight. "I. . ."

"Shhh, child," June said. "You tell us all about it in the morning. There's extra blankets in the closet. You show her those, Matthew."

Matthew made a noise of agreement, but mostly he was assuring himself that it was only a few hours until daylight. After breakfast—an early breakfast—he'd send this woman packing.

three

"You sleep okay, honey?" Mrs. Patrick had the same wide, generous smile as Kiera. Tall and slender, she also had the same strong facial bone structure and blue eyes. Only Mrs. Patrick's looked at her from behind a pair of oversized wire-framed glasses.

"Yes, thank you." Celie stepped into the large farm-style kitchen. She had slept well—sort of, when she wasn't lying in the big four-poster bed listening to the sound of the rain and trying not to worry about things. God had always provided for her, but she knew she was in big trouble with George Marcus Designs. When Libby Ellman discovered Celie had ignored company policy and taken home a gown, the head designer would be furious.

"Come have a seat." Mrs. Patrick patted the wooden chair next to her at the big, rectangular table. "Hope you like oatmeal." She gestured to Matthew, standing in front of a white range, stirring the contents of a large pot.

"I love it," Celie said, studying the straight line of Matthew's back. He was a tall man, muscular but not heavyset. He had thick, chestnut-colored hair more wavy than straight. His green flannel shirt and jeans looked comfortably worn, but there was nothing warm about the look he shot over his shoulder at her.

"It'll be ready in a minute," he said.

The room was clean and spacious—at least four times the size of Celie's galley-style kitchen in Stamford. The appliances looked old but fit well with the pine cabinets and butcher-block counters. A cheerful array of herbs sat in a bay window above the kitchen sink. Everything looked right, but something didn't feel right. Celie crossed her arms. Maybe it

17

was just her, but the room felt a little cold.

The hairless dog, Toaster, leaped from Mrs. Patrick's lap and rushed over to greet her. She bent to pet him, glad for the warmth of his skin against her hands.

"Come sit, Celie." Mrs. Patrick patted the space next to her.

Celie moved aside Mrs. Patrick's metal walker and took a seat at the table.

"Oatmeal's ready." Matthew pulled three bowls from a cabinet. The clattering china sounded angry. He didn't look at her as he set a bowl in front of her. Well, showing up in the middle of the night probably hadn't earned her any popularity points.

"The rain's stopped," June commented. "You're lucky you got through last night, Celie. Doesn't take much to make the McGillis pond overflow."

"There was a lot of water on the road," Celie agreed, "but I just kept driving."

She'd been terrified, gripping the wheel and leaning forward, struggling to see more clearly. A couple of times she'd heard water scraping the bottom of the car, but she'd just kept going, praying she wouldn't miss one of the signs pointing to the Patrick Orchards.

She hadn't seen the orchard last night, but she could see the trees now, acres and acres of them, visible through a large bay window. The sun had just come up enough for her to see trees filling the landscape, their gnarled and bare limbs gracefully posed as far as her eyes could see.

"Coffee, dear?"

"No thank you, Mrs. Patrick."

"Tea, then? That's what I'm drinking."

Celie's gaze swung to Matthew, who glared back at her.

"I'd love some tea, if it's not too much trouble."

"We don't have any of those fancy tea blends," Matthew said, ladling oatmeal into their bowls. "All we've got is plain old Lipton."

Even across the room, she could see the deep blue of his

irises. Kiera's were the same color, but unlike his sister, there was no friendly twinkle in them. "I love Lipton."

Matthew's mouth twisted as if he doubted this very much, but he put the kettle on the cooktop. Returning to the table, he blessed the meal and picked up his spoon.

"So tell us, dear, about the fire."

Celie's mind jumped to the crackling flames, the foul black smoke, and the horror of watching her home burn. She couldn't begin to describe it. "It was awful. Nobody knew what to do, where to go. . . ." She twisted her fingers together as she described the burly firemen in oxygen masks, the charred face of the ruined apartment building, the blank and lost expressions of her former neighbors, the terrible smell of acrid smoke.

June stroked her dog. "Oh, Celie, I'm so sorry."

She stirred her oatmeal. "At least no one was killed," she said. "Everyone got out."

"Thank God," June declared.

"Yes," Celie echoed. "He kept everyone safe."

June squeezed Celie's arm with a thin but surprisingly strong grasp. "Whatever we can do to help, we will. Please feel free to borrow Kiera's clothing or mine. Anything you need."

"I appreciate that, Mrs. Patrick. That's really nice of you. Just letting me stay last night was a blessing." Celie nibbled at her oatmeal then set the spoon in the bowl.

"Please call me June. Kiera has told us so much about you that I feel like I know you already. She loves your designs. Half her closet is filled with your clothing."

"Or used to be," Matthew said pointedly. "I think she took most of *those outfits* with her to Mexico."

The way he said "those outfits" made Celie's chin lift. She wanted to ask him just what was wrong with her outfits but then held her tongue. Now wasn't the time to start an argument. She focused on the last part of his statement. "You said Kiera was in Mexico?"

"Well, on her way," June said firmly. A look that Celie didn't understand passed between the two Patricks. "She's taking a cruise ship out of Florida."

"I'm surprised she didn't mention the cruise to me." Kiera tended to be impulsive. "Let's be spontaneous" was her battle cry. But usually Kiera told her everything—then again, Kiera had been pretty upset with her the last time they'd spoken.

"Wallace Blake dumped her," Matthew stated bluntly. "Left her a text message. Didn't even have the decency to tell her face-to-face."

"What?" Celie set her mug down. "He did what?"

"He also gave the modeling job she wanted to another girl—one he's now dating. I'm surprised she didn't tell you," Matthew said. "You being her best friend and all."

Celie dropped her gaze. Matthew was right. Kiera should have called her—and would have if Celie hadn't called Wallace Blake a player and warned her that he wasn't the kind of guy to stick around. Kiera's response had been to slam down the phone. That had been about two weeks ago. It was longer than they'd ever gone without speaking, but Celie had been so wrapped up in work she hadn't had time to fix things between them.

"When is she coming back?"

"We're not really sure," June said. "A couple of weeks, we think. I know she would want you to stay with us, Celie, until things get settled with your apartment."

Matthew set his spoon down. "I'm sure Celie has to get back to the city."

Kiera on a cruise, brokenhearted. The fire. The burned hand-painted silk and her own lost designs. Her future at George Marcus. Celie put her hands flat on the table as if that would keep her mind from spinning. She'd yet to call her parents or work. She didn't know which was worse—telling her parents or Libby Ellman about the fire. Her mother had been packing and repacking her suitcase for a straight month and would be tremendously disappointed. Crushed, really.

And Libby Ellman. Celie shuddered. Libby was going to kill her. *Please God, help me handle both of them.*

"Thank you for the offer, June, but I can't stay. I really need to get back to the city. May I use your phone before I leave?"

Matthew smiled for the first time since she'd walked into the room. He gestured toward a hallway off the kitchen. "Absolutely. You can use the one in my office."

ۿ

As soon as Celie left the room to make the necessary calls, Matthew said, "Don't you know who that is?"

His mother moved the half-eaten bowl of oatmeal closer so Toaster could lick its contents. "Of course I know who she is."

Matthew frowned as the small dog lapped up the contents. "You need to be eating more, Mom. If you want your hip to heal, you need the calcium in that oatmeal."

"My hip will heal, or it won't," she replied as if she didn't care one way or another. Matthew's stomach tightened the way it always did when she got like this, embracing the idea that this injury was the beginning of a slow downhill slide.

"If it weren't for her, Kiera would be here, with us. She never would have met that Wallace guy, and she'd never have gotten her heart broken."

"You don't know that, Matthew."

"She introduced them at a business party. Don't you remember Kiera telling us?"

"Maybe. It doesn't really matter."

"A girl like Celie is trouble."

"I like her."

Matthew pulled the oatmeal bowl right out from under Toaster's nose. He ignored the wistful look the dog gave him.

"You ought to help me convince Celie to stay," his mom added, giving him a look as unbending as steel. "If Kiera hears that her friend is staying with us, maybe she'll come home earlier."

Matthew set the dishes in the sink and turned on the faucet. When he'd driven Kiera to the airport, she'd given him a long hug, probably the longest she'd ever given him, and a look that said she wasn't coming back soon.

He'd always been able to fix things for Kiera—the china shepherdess that had fallen from her dresser, the frayed rope on the tire swing that she'd worn out, the first dent she'd put in their mom's old, blue Buick.

Matthew set a dish in the drying rack. "Let it go."

"Excuse me," Celie said quietly. He turned. She stood framed in the arched entranceway; her face was as white as her frilly blouse. "I was wondering if your offer was still open." She paused and swallowed. A bit dramatically, he thought. "I'd love to stay a few days with you all."

"Of course," his mother said, shooting him a triumphant look. "We'd love it."

"Thank you," Celie said, and her eyes shimmered with tears.

If she cried, he'd throw water on her. The water pressure in the sink was pretty good, and the spray from the hose might well cross the room. She was acting. Taking advantage of his mother's hospitality. Just like she'd taken advantage of Kiera's tendency to see the good in people. Celie was a good actress but an actress all the same. He wasn't buying it.

"Will you tell us what happened, honey?"

"Yes," Matthew echoed but made little effort to conceal the skepticism in his voice. "What happened?"

"She fired me," Celie said, and her lips quivered. She covered her mouth with her hand and looked embarrassed.

"She fired you," Matthew prompted.

"I took a dress home from the store, and I wasn't supposed to." Celie's breath hitched, and her cheeks flushed. "I was trying to fix it in time for the fashion show, but. . ." She sighed—again a bit too dramatically, he thought. "It got burned up. And so did three other dresses that were supposed to be in the show—my designs." She blinked hard. "Libby said I would be lucky if they didn't press charges against me."

"Oh, honey," his mother said in her most sympathetic

voice. "She sounds like a horrible person. It wasn't your fault a fire burned down the building."

"Yes, but I shouldn't have taken a dress home without clearing it with Libby. George Marcus—he's the owner of the business—is really strict about us doing that. It's a security thing. He doesn't want anyone seeing his designs until he's ready."

"Well, he sounds like a horrible person, too," his mother said.

Matthew turned on the faucet. His mother hadn't seemed to grasp the concept that Celie had done something wrong—practically stealing from the company—and had gotten fired for it. Clearly they were getting stuck with Celie, at least for a few days. He refused to be part of this new drama. As far as he was concerned, the sooner Celie left, the better.

four

Celie set the grocery bags on the kitchen table. She found June in the living room, gently snoring in a reclining chair of blue velvet fabric. The hairless dog, Toaster, sprawled across her lap, and the television droned on in the background.

Celie tiptoed away. Good. June probably needed to rest after last night. Returning to the kitchen, Celie began dinner. As well as a few clothing and personal essentials, she'd picked up some chicken breasts at a cute little general store in town.

She found a glass baking dish in one of the lower cabinets and pulled a frying pan with a shiny copper bottom from a hook on the wall. She seared the meat in the frying pan and made a glaze out of some peach jam.

Toaster came in to watch. When he began whining at the back door, she figured he needed to go out. She reached for her trench coat and opened the door.

The bald little dog dashed ahead of her, happily watering a bush, then refused to come back when she called.

Celie grabbed her coat and ran out the door. She chased Toaster through a grove of medium-sized trees—apple trees, no doubt—and ground her teeth in frustration when the dog refused to let her catch him.

What's going on, God? I've lost my house, my job, and now I can't even catch a dog?

Toaster led her to a big red barn. From the Dutch door of a front-facing stall, a horse greeted her with a low-pitched rumble. She was just about to pat its head when Toaster began yipping. Celie hurried to investigate.

Behind the barn, three small goats stood in the middle of a grassy pasture area. They were facing off with Toaster. Celie shouted for the dog to come, but, of course, he ignored her.

24

She didn't like the way the biggest goat was pawing the ground. Its horns looked capable of turning Toaster into doggy shish kebab. She shouted at Toaster, but the dog didn't seem to realize the goat meant business.

Celie's heart thumped as she swung her legs over the fence and dropped lightly into the paddock. The enclosed area had not seemed so big from the fence, but now it seemed like miles. She was almost to the little dog now; all she had to do was reach down and grab his bouncy little body. She reached for him, and then, as if by some unknown signal, the horned goat charged.

Celie screamed, turned tail, and ran for her life. Toaster shot past her. Her Jimmy Choos weren't designed for running across a pasture, but Celie had no choice. Her trench coat tore as she reached the fence line and jumped. Safe on the other side of the fence, Toaster trotted up to her, panting as if he were about to hyperventilate. Celie scooped him up. "Troublemaker," she whispered. Toaster licked her face enthusiastically.

"You're faster than I thought."

Celie spun around. Matthew stood behind her, and judging from his broad smile, he'd seen the whole thing. "Which is fortunate for me," Celie snapped. She shifted the dog in her arms. "You should post a sign warning people the goats are dangerous."

"Your life was never in danger," Matthew said. A very slight breeze lifted his wavy, chestnut hair. "Happy isn't an attack goat. The only thing that was ever in danger was the buttons on your coat."

"You obviously didn't see *Happy* charging me. He would have *horned* me if he'd caught me."

"You mean, butted you." There was the smallest twitch at the corner of his mouth that could have been a smile. "And you were moving much too fast. Never knew anyone could run in fancy shoes like those."

"It's not like I had a lot of choice," Celie snapped. "Besides, it just proves that you can wear Jimmy Choos anywhere."

Celie glanced down at her boots, stained with mud but still lovely. Even on sale they'd cost her a week's paycheck. But they were worth every penny. A less-quality heel would have snapped under that kind of stress.

"Next time you take Toaster for a walk, you need to put him on a leash." Matthew's voice had taken on a definitely stern quality.

Celie nodded.

"And he needs to wear a coat," Matthew continued. "There's a dog coat in the mudroom. A dog that has no hair is very sensitive to cold weather."

Celie held the dog a fraction closer. She could feel the dog's heart beating rapidly. "You think he'll be okay?"

"Yeah, but you'd better take him back to the house. I'll be down after I finish closing up the barn."

Celie hurried back to the house, hoping that Toaster hadn't gotten chilled. They hadn't been at the barn long, but the sun had started to set. The air felt much colder than when she'd left the house earlier. She walked quickly through the trees. In the distance, she heard the wind moving through the valley, and seconds later it sliced through her coat. Toaster shivered, so she opened her coat and slipped him inside. He snuggled against her like a baby.

Another gust of wind moved through the orchards, a dull, strong roar that burned her ears and carried with it, she thought, the ever-so-faint smell of something sweet, like roses.

five

After dinner Matthew washed the dishes and Celie dried them. As he handed Celie a dish, he thought of Kiera and the countless times they'd stood at the porcelain sink doing dishes. It'd only been two days since she left, but he couldn't stop worrying about her. He still couldn't believe she'd tossed her cell phone out the window of her car as she'd driven away. That hadn't seemed like a very rational thing to do, but then again none of her recent decisions had been rational.

Kiera'd always been a bit impulsive, but a cruise to Cozumel seemed over the top, even for her. If his father had been alive, Matthew wondered what he would have done.

One of Matthew's strongest memories of his father was when Matthew was six years old. They had been taking down a tree with blight—it had unexpectedly split in half, trapping one of the workers beneath. Matthew's father had single-handedly lifted the trunk off Eustis Jones—a feat that Matthew later heard should have taken at least two men. When he'd asked his father about it, Dermott Patrick had simply said, "You take care of your own. You find a way to do what you have to do."

He'd tried. He'd been doing pretty well until Wallace Blake came along and lured Kiera away. Before Wallace, Kiera had been dating Aaron Buckman, his best friend since kindergarten. Aaron was quiet and steady, a strong Christian who ran the True Value hardware store. Matthew had foreseen many enjoyable family dinners with them.

A gust of wind rattled the windows. The last breath of winter. He passed the dripping plate to Celie. If the *Farmer's Almanac* was correct, and it usually was, the trees would be budding soon. He'd call Sue Enderman and set a date for the bees.

"You sure Toaster's okay?" Celie asked, casting an anxious glance at the dog in his mother's lap.

His mom stroked the little dog. "Toastie's fine. It's not the first time he's chased those goats. Right, Matthew?"

He nodded. "You can stand two feet away, bellow that dog's name at the top of your lungs, and he pretends he doesn't hear you."

Celie shot Matthew a sympathetic glance, which he pretended not to notice.

"You have to be nicer to him, Matthew. He likes cheeseburgers. If you started giving him cheeseburgers when you called him, he'd come running." She scratched behind the dog's upright ears. "Wouldn't you, little Toastie?"

"If I started making him cheeseburgers, his belly would be scraping the floor, which it nearly is already. You have to stop feeding him so much, Mom."

"But that chicken was simply delicious," June said. "Celie will have to tell you how to make it."

As he rinsed the plate, Celie babbled enthusiastically about herbs and searing a crust. It sounded a lot more complicated than the store-bought barbecue sauce he usually used. Celie happily finished the recipe, concluding that she and June would have to shop together at Tom's Market.

His mother's smile vanished abruptly. "I really don't get out of the house much anymore." She gestured to the walker. "Lugging that ugly thing around is a real pain in the neck."

The china plate clacked gently as Celie set it in the cupboard. "You know, we could decorate it. Put some cheerful ribbons on it or spray paint it hot pink."

Matthew finished the last dish and turned off the faucet. "Or Mom could do the exercises the doctor gave her and get stronger."

"As far as I am concerned, the Radio City Music Hall Rockettes would find those stretches challenging."

"The point, Mom, is to work at them. You'll get more flexible the more you do them."

His mother snorted.

"I could help," Celie volunteered. "We'll put on some good music, and it'll be fun."

Although his mom agreed, Matthew doubted it'd ever happen. He'd tried countless times, even gotten down on the floor, demonstrating how easy they were to do. His mother had nearly split her sides laughing as Toaster had licked his face and then sat on his chest.

He set the sponge in its holder and retreated to his office.

⸙

"Paperwork," June sighed as she settled herself into the velvet fabric of the reclining chair. "The computer is supposed to make it easier, but all it does is complicate things."

June patted her lap, and Toaster jumped onto her. Reaching for the television remote, she punched a button.

"We use computers all the time for designing," Celie said, "but you're right. I much prefer to draw by hand." She sat back on a rather formal sofa with a lovely blue and white chintz fabric. She'd asked June if she could borrow a sewing basket, and now Celie searched for a needle and thread to repair her torn coat.

Just the act of holding the needle in her fingers soothed her, as if she were repairing not just the fabric but also something deep within herself. She kept the tension even, and soon a neat line of tiny stitches formed. Looking up, she found June watching her. "Do you sew?"

The old woman nodded. "Oh, I used to. There's a fabulous fabric store in town called Fabric Attic." She pointed to a set of plain white curtains flanking the windows. "I made those, too." She smiled wryly. "About a hundred years ago."

"They're pretty."

"Oh, they're pretty plain. Every once in a while, I think about redecorating, but then it seems too much work."

"Your home is beautiful. That wing chair in the corner and that secretary on the wall— they're antiques, aren't they?"

"Yes, from Ireland. Matthew's grandfather Thomas brought

them over when he immigrated in 1922. He built this house—no plumbing or electricity back then—but lots of land to farm. They started with vegetables." June paused and took a breath. "Don't get me started. I could talk for hours about the orchards."

"I'd love to hear more."

June was only too willing to oblige. Before Celie knew it, the trench coat was mended and June was deep into a story about the depression and how relatives from Danbury, Connecticut, had come to the farm because it was their only source of food. "There was always enough here," June concluded proudly. "Thank the Lord."

"Mom?"

Celie jumped at the sound of Matthew's deep voice. She hadn't realized he was there, standing with his arms folded beneath the arch of the entrance, and she had no idea how long he'd been there.

"Getting late," he said. "We get up early here."

Celie bristled. Just because she was a city girl didn't mean she didn't get up early. Plus, he'd practically come in and flipped off the light switch. The decision about when to go to bed should have been up to June.

"Okay, dear," June said. "Go on, Toastie. Go to Matthew."

The little dog jumped to the ground with a light thump. Matthew slipped a worn quilted jacket over the dog's body and clipped on Toaster's leash. "Be right back."

"He's a good man," June said, staring at the place her son had been. "Don't know what I'd do without him."

He might be a good man, but he wasn't a particularly friendly one. "Kiera said he was a big teddy bear."

June chuckled. "That sounds like her." A wistful expression passed over her features. "Maybe she'll call tomorrow."

"Maybe," Celie echoed, wishing that she had not mentioned her friend's name at all. As June continued to perch on the edge of the chair, Celie added, "Is there something I can do to help you?"

June shook her head. "No, honey, I'm fine."

A moment later Matthew and Toaster returned, the chill of the night still clinging to Matthew's thick wool sweater. "Celie," Matthew said as Toaster dashed between her and June, greeting them as if he'd been away for hours and not minutes, "can you bring the walker?"

She wasn't sure what he meant, but then it became clear as Matthew scooped June into his arms and carried her to the staircase. *Oh.* With her bad hip, she probably couldn't manage the stairs by herself.

The wooden steps rose in a straight, steep climb, but Matthew climbed them all without pausing. His breathing didn't change, either. If it hadn't been for the way his muscles strained beneath the tight stretch of his sweater, Celie might have thought it required no effort on his part at all.

On the landing, Matthew gently set his mother down and kept a steadying hand on her elbow as Celie placed the walker in front of her. June thanked them both. "Good night, then," she said and started down the hallway.

"Good night," Celie echoed. "Sleep well."

Matthew watched June make her way down the hallway, but Celie watched him. The overhead light illuminated the grooves forming along the straight line of his mouth, the way his chestnut hair waved where it touched the top of his ear, the faintest trace of a tan line just visible beneath the collar of his shirt.

He turned suddenly, and she dropped her gaze, embarrassed to have been caught staring at him. She studied his stocking-clad feet, the fabric all but worn away at his big toe. He obviously cared more about taking care of June, the house, and the orchards than he did himself.

"Good night, Celie," Matthew said formally. "See you at breakfast." The corners of his mouth tugged ever so slightly. "Six a.m."

Was he mocking her? His eyes sparkled with unspoken challenge. It had to be the whole city-girl thing. As if she somehow wasn't tough enough to get up early in the morning. She felt the tender feelings she'd started to have toward him drain away. He had no idea how hard it was to ride a packed subway in high heels or deal with a boss who could skewer you verbally just for saying good morning if the caffeine in her morning cappuccino hadn't kicked in yet.

Matthew had no idea how tough a city girl had to be. Not yet. But she'd show him.

six

The next morning, Celie slipped into the jeans she'd bought in town and a turtleneck sweater. She accessorized the outfit with a colorful silk scarf she found in Kiera's closet and, of course, her trusty Jimmy Choo ankle boots. The wooden stairs creaked under her weight as she tiptoed through the dark, silent house. A single light burned in the kitchen. No sign of Matthew. Good.

She put a filter in the coffee pot and filled the tank with several cups of water. A large pot hung from a hook on the wall, and she set it on the counter.

As a child, Celie had spent two weeks every summer with her maternal grandmother, Rosemary McMullin, in Dennis, Massachusetts, a small town just south of Cape Cod Bay. Nanna had loved cooking and spent hours teaching her all the family recipes.

It didn't take long to find the right ingredients, and soon the hot cereal bubbled away on the range. She turned to the table next, scrubbed clean from last night and completely bare of anything but the shine of its wood. It needed a tablecloth or a runner—something to give the room a little more color.

An old maple dresser with pretty lines and tarnished brass knobs sat against the sidewall. When she opened one of the drawers, she found a stack of neatly folded linens. She selected the one on top—a spring green cloth with lace edging.

The material was creased, as if it hadn't been used for a long time, but its dimensions fit the table exactly. As she smoothed it flat, she noticed a dark stain in one corner and a hole in another. After breakfast she'd clean and mend it.

She found a pair of silver candlesticks in the dining room and placed them on the kitchen table. Standing back, she smiled at the effect. Stunning, really. Warm and inviting, too. She'd light the candles when Matthew came downstairs.

She was just finishing cutting up some apples and oranges when the door of the mudroom opened and Matthew came in, along with a rush of cold air. He took off his boots and walked into the room. His gaze went from the table to Celie's face. "What in the world is going on?"

"I'm making breakfast for you and June," Celie said. "It's my way of thanking you for letting me stay here." She gestured toward the blue ceramic coffee mug. "You like your coffee with milk, no sugar, right?"

He just stared, and she wondered what was wrong, then June's voice called softly from the top of the stairs. As Matthew hurried to bring her downstairs, Celie poured June's tea.

When June saw the table, she covered her mouth with her hands, and her blue eyes grew large behind her bifocal lenses. "It's so beautiful." She turned to Matthew in excitement. "It's like a banquet for a queen."

Celie beamed. "Sit down, Your Highness, and I'll serve you breakfast. If you're ready, that is."

Matthew folded his arms. "I'm ready for you to put it all back. Right now."

"Put back what?" Celie read anger in the tight set of his jaw. His response made no sense, no sense at all.

"The linen tablecloth. That is a family heirloom. It isn't something you use."

Heirloom? Celie looked from Matthew's angry face to June's smiling one. "I didn't know. I'm sorry. It was in the dresser with a lot of other tablecloths. I just assumed. . ."

"You assumed wrong." Matthew narrowed his gaze.

"I'm sorry. I'll put it right back."

"And those candlesticks," he added, managing, without raising his voice, to sound tremendously intimidating. "They belong in the dining room."

"Okay, okay. I get the picture." She stepped toward the table, intending to get right to work putting things back, then tripped over Toaster. She saw the kitchen table flying toward her and put her hands out to break her fall. Then somehow Matthew was in front of her, catching her right before she crashed into the table.

He staggered as she fell against him. The juice glass sloshed but didn't fall over, and then all she could see was the hard wall of his chest. He straightened but continued to hold her. "And that's exactly why we don't use that tablecloth," Matthew said as she stepped back from him. "If you'd knocked into the table, you'd have spilled everything everywhere."

Celie stepped away. As Matthew started to follow, something in his back pocket caught on the lace edging. Before he realized what had happened, he jerked the tablecloth. The juice pitcher crashed over, dumping its orange river across the table. Matthew's coffee cup sailed off the table edge, along with a bowl of fruit and a pitcher of cream. The mug shattered as it hit the ground.

Worst of all—the old linen tablecloth lay in a bath of coffee, milk, and juice.

Celie knew she should run for a towel or unhook the tablecloth from Matthew's pocket or upright the fallen dishes. However, the horror of it all had her feet rooted to the ground.

June started applauding then, and when Celie's disbelieving gaze turned to her, she began laughing. June pointed to the tablecloth still attached to Matthew's back pocket, tried to say something, then lost it to another round of laughter. "Wha—Wha—What do you do for your next trick, Matthew?" she managed finally. "Pull a ra–ha–ha–ha—rabbit out of your hat?"

Matthew shot her a dark look. "This isn't funny." He unhooked the tablecloth and righted the fallen juice pitcher.

"It's very funny," June corrected, pausing as another round of laughter shook her. "You're just being stodgy."

She hooted with laughter. Toaster began licking the puddle forming beneath the kitchen table. Celie came to life and gathered up the soaked tablecloth and brought it to the sink.

She held the fabric beneath the cold water. Her knees felt weak. "Do you have any baking soda? Sometimes it lifts the stains out."

"In the pantry," June said, wiping her eyes. "Oh golly. If I'd only had a camera. The look on your face, Matthew. It was something to behold."

"You should see your face right now," Matthew countered. "Like a beefsteak tomato."

June let out her breath along with another hearty chuckle. With effort, she gathered herself and stood very stiff and straight. "This is why we don't use that tablecloth," she said in an impressive imitation of her son. She lapsed into another series of whooping noises.

"It's coming out," Celie announced with relief as she rinsed the cloth.

"Oh who cares?" June wiped her streaming eyes. "I haven't laughed like that in a coon's age."

"I know," Matthew replied. His gaze shifted from June to Celie, and something flickered in his eyes. The anger was gone, and he was smiling a bit sheepishly.

Celie helped pick up the rest of the mess, working silently with him, but every now and then, she'd look up and find he was looking at her. Each time their gazes met, something stirred inside her, a little shivery feeling. When Matthew wasn't glaring at her, he sure was handsome.

Yesterday the kitchen had seemed cold and a little lacking in something, although she hadn't known just what. She remembered her mother saying cheerfully how sometimes it took a good mess to get things cleaned up.

"Is the oatmeal ready?" June commented from her supervisory seat at the table. "Hope you made a lot. Toastie and I are hungry."

seven

"It's here!" June cried.

Celie didn't have to ask what "it" was. Around two o'clock every day, June took up a post at the window and didn't move until the mail arrived.

June let the living room drapery fall back, and the room dimmed slightly with the loss of light. She turned to Celie. "I have a good feeling about today."

June had been saying the same thing ever since Celie had arrived at the orchards, and every day she slumped with disappointment when the mail failed to bring news of Kiera. Clipping a leash to Toaster's collar, Celie headed for the front door. *One small postcard, a note, anything from Kiera. Please, God.*

The sun warmed Celie's cheeks as she hurried down the Patricks' long, tree-lined driveway. In the twelve days since she'd arrived, the trees had formed small green buds, tightly wrapped along the wiry ends of their branches. The angle of the sun seemed higher, the light flowing through the trees stronger.

Please, God, let a note from Kiera arrive today, she repeated as Toaster playfully jumped up and took the blue nylon leash in his teeth.

She grabbed the contents of the box and rushed back to the house. June searched the pile eagerly, making no effort to hide her sigh of disappointment when she failed to find any communication from Kiera. "Oh well," she said. "Maybe tomorrow." She handed Celie a long, cream-colored envelope. "But there's something for you."

The return address said HECKMAN AND ERLIS and bore a Hartford, Connecticut, address. Celie ripped the edges and pulled out two slim sheets of paper. She skimmed the contents of the letter and looked at the check.

From her seat across the kitchen table, June said, "Everything all right, dear?"

"Yes." Celie folded up the papers and stuck them back in the envelope. "It's the check from the insurance company."

"That came very fast, didn't it?" June flipped indifferently through an L.L.Bean catalog. "We had a terrible time getting the insurance company to pay when one of the cold barns—that's where we store the apples after we pick them—got hit by lightning. Matthew had to call several times to straighten everything out."

Celie fingered the slender envelope. It seemed strange to think she held the sum of her life in her hands, that everything she'd owned could be reduced to numbers on a thin, unsubstantial piece of paper. She could rip the check into tiny pieces and watch the wind carry it off, and then she would be left with nothing.

"You look a little sad, honey." June lowered the catalog and studied Celie's face. "If that check isn't the right amount, we'll get Matthew to call. They'll listen to him."

Celie shook her head. "It isn't that." She forced herself to smile reassuringly at June. "I guess it finally sinking in—the fire and everything being gone." She sighed. "I guess I'm a little sad about leaving, too. You've been so good to me, June. I really appreciate it."

June leaned forward, her blue eyes troubled. "Leaving? Who said anything about leaving?"

"I can't impose on you forever." Celie'd been praying for a miracle, a divine intervention—something that involved Libby Ellman calling on the telephone, her voice oozing apology. "Milah told us everything. There's been a terrible misunderstanding," she'd say. "We need you back here." However, according to James—who didn't know the full story, either—Celie had a better chance of getting hit by lightning than she did of getting her job back at George Marcus.

"But where will you go, Celie?"

Restless, Celie stood. "Centerville, a little south of Dayton, Ohio. My parents have a dry cleaning business there. You want some tea?"

"Yes, thank you. But, Celie, dry cleaning? Why not get another job as a designer? There's got to be plenty of companies that would hire you."

Celie filled the kettle with tap water. "When I went to work for George Marcus, I signed a nondisclosure agreement. It said if I were dismissed that I couldn't work for a competitor for one year." She shrugged. "It was supposed to protect the company against corporate espionage. I never dreamed I'd be fired."

"If you ask me, you're better off without them. I've seen your fashions, and you have a real gift for design."

"I messed up. I shouldn't have taken that dress home without permission."

"I'm sure you had a good reason."

Celie thought about Milah. "It really doesn't matter now."

June clucked sympathetically. "You really want to go back there, don't you?"

"It was my dream job."

"Then you've got to get it back."

The teakettle whistled. Celie pulled two ceramic mugs from the cabinet. "I think that door has closed."

June seemed to consider this for a moment. "God could open it."

"What if God wants me in Ohio?"

"Then you'll end up in Ohio, Celie," June said firmly. "God puts us right where He wants us. And there's a reason you're here and not in Ohio. If He's given you a dream to be a fashion designer—and I think He has—then maybe you need to stay right where you are. Why don't you use that insurance money to sew a dress so amazing your boss will have no choice but to hire you back?"

Celie let the tea steep. She thought about her mother seated at her sewing machine in the small nook just off the cash register. Day after day, year after year, her mom worked on altering and repairing garments that came into the dry cleaners. She never complained, but Celie knew she'd once dreamed of being a designer herself. An early marriage and Celie's birth had put those dreams on hold. The day before Celie had left for New York, her mother had thrown a party, and later that night, she'd pressed a check for a thousand dollars into her hands. "I'm so proud of you," she whispered.

Celie heard the thump of the metal walker on the hardwood floor and the softer, scuttling noise of Toaster, then she felt a warm hand touch her shoulder. "You're welcome to stay here, Celie, as long as you like. I'm not saying you'll have enough money to recreate all the dresses you lost in the fire, but you'll have enough to do what you need. God will see to that."

Celie didn't want to go back to Ohio a failure, but she didn't want to impose herself on the Patricks, either. Plus she had bills to pay—those would eat up a lot of the insurance money—and if she sewed anything, it was going to be another hand-painted silk dress like the one that had gotten her into this trouble in the first place. "I appreciate your offer, but I don't want to impose on you all."

June laughed. "You aren't imposing at all. I'd welcome your company."

"It would take me at least a month to sew those dresses."

"All the better," June said. "You'll be here when Kiera comes home. She should be back by then, don't you think?"

"I hope so. But what about Matthew? I don't think he'd be too happy if I stayed."

"You just concentrate on the designing. I'll handle Matthew. Do you know how to make chicken dumplings? No?" Her silver eyebrows lifted. Behind her lenses, her eyes sparkled. "Well don't worry, I'll show you."

eight

Matthew heard the music before he even stepped into the house. Someone was playing his stereo full volume, and it wasn't hard to guess just who, either. He hung his coat on a peg in the mudroom and unlaced the damp laces of his work boots.

The smell of something delicious assaulted his senses, distracting him momentarily from the loud music. He took another deep breath and felt his stomach practically flip with hunger.

His mood improved a notch. He'd spent the day working on the malfunctioning air-conditioning unit in the south barn and still couldn't get the storage area below thirty-four degrees. It wasn't an issue right now, but leaving a job unfinished always bothered him.

He lifted the lid on a black, cast iron pot on the gas range. Chicken and dumplings. His mouth watered.

"In the Blink of an Eye" started to play. He followed the notes into the living room and paused beneath the arched entranceway. The coffee table had been pushed back, and all the cushions from the couch were on the floor. His mother lay flat on her back on top of the cushions with Toaster draped over her hips like a doggy heating pad.

His mother was doing leg lifts—the very exercises the doctor had been telling her to do for months. Celie, kneeling by his mom's side, helped raise his mother's leg a few inches above the ground. "That's it!" Celie said, sounding as excited as if they'd just discovered the cure for cancer. "That's it! One more and then we'll rest."

"One more," his mother said dryly, "and I'll be dead."

But she made that last lift and with Celie's help sat up.

Each woman positively beamed with pride.

He looked at Celie. How had she done it? He retreated before she saw him. Then, and only then, did he let himself grin. The music continued—and so did their voices, singing along. Both of them about as off-key as he'd ever heard. His mother's alto was as flat as the tire on the wheelbarrow, and Celie missed a high note by about a mile.

Peals of laughter—Celie's and then his mom's—floated in from the living room. He sat down at the old wooden table. How long since the house had been filled with that sound? He couldn't remember. *Maybe never*, he thought.

&

His mom ate every bite of dinner. She said the exercises had given her an appetite. Matthew took shameless advantage of her high spirits and kept adding dumplings to her plate. She'd always been slender but never as thin as now. She seemed so fragile to him lately, like a twig that'd snap under the least bit of pressure. He thought if he could fatten her up that she'd be stronger.

He glanced at Celie, who'd also put a good dent in the dumplings. She liked to eat. She was curvy but not heavy, and he wondered just where she was putting it. He realized then that both Celie and June were staring at him, and the room had gone silent. "What?"

"I just asked you twice, Matthew," his mother said, "about your day."

"Not much," he said. "Usual stuff. Your goat"—he paused to give June a significant look—"jumped in the wheelbarrow this morning when I was cleaning the stall. Wouldn't get out, either." He forked a dumpling in half and anticipated June's reaction.

"Happy used to do that all the time with me," his mother agreed. "Stand there like he was king of the world. You should see him, Celie."

"Only from behind the fence," Celie said. "I have no desire to be shish kebab for a goat."

Matthew chuckled. "Those horns aren't meant for impaling. They're used for flipping."

"That makes me feel so much better." Celie rolled her eyes dramatically. "I'd so much rather somersault over Happy's back and have him trample on top of me."

She winked at him, and Matthew winked back before he could stop himself. He chewed another bite of dumpling and ordered himself to stop looking at her.

Yesterday he'd tried to get his mother out of the house. He'd asked her to go to church with him and ended up with Celie instead. They'd arrived a little late and had squeezed into one of the back pews. He'd endured an hour and a half of sitting pressed tightly against her. She'd smelled very faintly of honey, and he'd been fascinated by the way one strand of her dark hair escaped the messy bun and curved around her pale cheek. Afterward, he realized, he could barely recall one word of the sermon.

Matthew set down his glass of milk and wiped his mouth with a napkin. "I'm going to True Value tomorrow. I need a part for the air conditioner in the south barn."

"Wonderful!" His mother beamed as if he'd just announced he held the winning lottery ticket. "Celie needs to go to town, too. I'm sure you won't mind taking her."

"It's okay," Celie said quickly. "I can drive myself. I don't know how long I'll be, and—"

"That's ridiculous," his mom interrupted, ignoring the frantic appeal that had to be clear in his eyes. "It'll give you both a chance to visit on the way. Celie came up with the most interesting plan this afternoon. Another dumpling, dear?"

Matthew had a bad feeling. His gaze swung to Celie who seemed to be exceptionally thirsty all of a sudden. "Plan? What plan? Maybe you'd better tell me now."

"Celie is going to be staying with us for a little while longer." His mom stabbed another dumpling. "She's going to use the insurance money to buy sewing supplies."

Celie set her glass down and gave him a tentative smile. "If it's okay with you, that is."

"Of course it's all right with Matthew," his mom said before he could disagree. She gave him a calculating look. "I don't think I could do my leg exercises without her."

Matthew recognized blackmail when he heard it. He also knew when his mother was bluffing and when she was serious. And she was serious. He put another dumpling on her plate. He knew a little bit about blackmail, too.

ã

The Fabric Attic was located on South Main Street, just past the Old Bethlehem Historical Society. He watched Celie's reaction as they pulled up to the old Victorian building.

"It's purple," she said. "How cute!"

"It is purple," he agreed.

Since childhood, the tall skinny house with yellow curlicue trim and long, narrow windows had always reminded Matthew of a Halloween house. He supposed it had something to do with the orange cat that was always curled in the window box and the bowl of candy that always sat next to the cash register.

The yellow door stuck and then creaked open as if he'd caused the house physical pain. "Welcome to the Fabric Attic," he said.

She stepped past him into the dim interior. "Oh Matthew, this place is so cool!"

He couldn't help but smile as she rushed past him to explore. *Like a kid at a candy store*, he thought as he followed her down aisle after aisle of floor-to-ceiling shelves containing fabrics of every color, texture, and pattern.

"Look at this," Celie declared, tugging at a bolt of gauzy blue fabric covered with tiny pearls. "This would make the coolest hat—all I'd need is a little velvet of the same color."

He lifted the fabric from the stack and watched her unwind a length and hold it against her head, grinning from ear to ear. The strong color set off her fair skin, and the sparkle in her eyes looked like light off water. He looked away, commenting on the first fabric that caught his eyes. "I like that blue plaid."

Celie grinned. "It just happens to be the exact plaid of the shirt you're wearing. Pick another fabric you like, and I'll make you a shirt."

Matthew glanced down. Sure enough, his flannel shirt matched the colors in the bolt just above his head. He grinned a bit sheepishly. "Thanks but no thanks." He pretended interest in a blue pattern with white palm trees. "Stick with the plan."

What there is of a plan, Matthew amended. Other than buying materials to replace the dresses that'd burned up in Celie's apartment, the plan was to walk around until one of the materials "spoke" to Celie. That was it. Depending on the fabric, she'd sew something and get her old job back. The whole way in the car, he'd tried to talk to her about studying the market, talking to potential buyers, or targeting a particular audience. All his ideas had been met with a polite, "No thank you."

"Is anything speaking to you yet?" He followed her down a long aisle filled with bolts of white and pale yellow fabrics. Who could have imagined, though, there would be so many shades? How could anyone make a choice?

"They're all talking to me." Celie shot him an amused glance. "Could you please reach that bolt of cream silk for me?"

She unwrapped a small portion, fingered the texture, then held it to the light. Shaking her head, she had him replace the fabric and then had him pull down another bolt, which looked exactly like the first one.

Her lips pursed, and her head cocked thoughtfully. "It doesn't have the embroidery on it, but it's a douppioni, and the shade of ivory is exactly right. It just might work. Now we need to find the right trim—and fabric paint."

Matthew blinked when he saw the cost per yard of the fabric—nearly fifty dollars a yard. He followed her into another department and watched as she filled a basket with additional supplies. Just how much was this dress going to cost?

She paused in another aisle in front of a bolt of frothy

pink fabric. Pulling it off the shelf, she sighed in pleasure and draped a length of it over her arm. She also bought a chocolate-colored shiny fabric with a tiny white floral print. A bolt of yellow silk joined the other fabrics on the worktable. As more bolts of fabric were added to the table, Matthew began to understand why his mother had wanted him to go along in the first place. Celie was going to need help carrying everything.

"That ought to do it," Celie announced, but she had her gaze on a bolt of green fabric.

The material was the color of moss. Just looking at it made him think of cool, silky things like river water flowing over stones. They both reached for the fabric at the same time, and their hands touched. He jerked back as if she'd stung him. But it hadn't hurt. Quite the opposite. He looked at her carefully. How had she done that? Had she felt it, too?

With pink cheeks, Celie looked at the price of the fabric and winced. She started to put the cloth back, but he stopped her.

"Hold on. I like that one," he said.

"Me, too." Celie replaced the fabric. "But it's too expensive."

"Put something else back, then. The pink one."

Celie shook her head. "That one doesn't cost very much, and I need the others." She looked once more at the green fabric. "Let's get going."

He hesitated. "Why don't you bring it over to the register? Maybe it's on sale or something."

It wasn't, though, and Celie went pale as the salesperson finished ringing up all her purchases. "Don't cut the green silk," she said. "I'll have to come back for it."

Don't do it, Matthew told himself. *Don't you get involved in this.* And then he heard himself say very clearly, "Well, how much extra would you need for that green silk?"

The salesperson named a sum. It was more cash than he had in his wallet. He really didn't have that kind of money to throw around on fabric, but something inside him was telling him to purchase it anyway. It made no sense, but the little voice in his head kept saying, *Go ahead, Matthew. You need to do this.* He needed to do this? Matthew didn't think so. He didn't even want to like Celie, much less help her. But the feeling in his gut was so strong that he found himself reaching for his wallet and pulling out the debit card.

He was an idiot. Just as bad as his sister and mother. He waved off her expressions of thanks and promises of paying him back. Yet looking at her face, he found himself unable to regret what he'd just done. He started to whistle as they carried the bags of sewing supplies back to the truck.

nine

"Come on, Toaster," Celie urged as the small dog paused for about the twentieth time to sniff a bush. "We've got work to do. The light is perfect."

The May sun bloomed high above her as she walked deeper into the grove of apple trees, her impatience with the dog replaced with a sense of wonder as she gazed at row upon row of apple trees. After spending the morning painting flowers on the ivory silk, it felt great to be outdoors. The branches had filled in with leaves now, and as Matthew had pointed out yesterday when they'd driven past the orchards on their way to the Fabric Attic, there were tiny, white blooms nestled in the arms of the trees.

Toaster stopped to sniff. With a resigned sigh, Celie opened her new sketchbook. She needed both hands to draw, so she dropped the dog's leash and stepped on it with the toe of her Jimmy Choo boot.

Better. She knew how to recreate the fashions lost in the apartment fire, but she still hadn't completely decided what to do with the green silk. Opening her sketchbook, she flipped past the drawings she'd made last night—preliminary sketches of possible dress designs—and moved to a fresh page. The tree in front of her had a nice triangular shape. She began to draw it, striving not so much for detail as to capture its raw bones, the patterns the leaves made against the branches.

She shifted her weight, leaning closer to study an oval-shaped leaf. The way it absorbed the light fascinated her, and she wanted to draw the light and dark tones as well as the veins.

Toaster must have sensed her distraction because the next

thing she knew, she was watching his brown body tear down the grass path between the rows of trees. The blue leash followed behind him like an afterthought.

Celie shouted the dog's name but wasn't surprised when Toaster didn't come or sit or stay or anything else she ordered. They ran deeper into the grove. The trees seemed to grow larger and thicker, the distances between them becoming greater. She spotted Toaster just ahead and slowed her steps so she wouldn't frighten him. "Toastie," she called, trying to make her voice sound as much like June's as possible. "You want a cheeseburger, little Toastie?"

The small dog looked suspicious but interested. Celie kept promising cheeseburgers, and the dog seemed to understand that word very well. "And you'll get one just as soon as we get home," she said, grabbing the end of the leash and sighing with relief.

She was just about to turn around when a tall, bushy apple tree caught her eye. Its leaves shone a brilliant silver yellow, reminding her of the color of the silk fabric she'd bought yesterday. Opening up her sketchbook, she began to draw. Her fingers tingled as she sketched, the way they always did when a good design started to take shape.

Excited, she studied the shadows in the trees and thought of how they might translate to draping the fabric. A slight breeze moved through the trees, and the entire tree seemed to shimmer before resettling. Celie's pencil paused as she wondered how to translate the movement.

Toaster growled. Celie looked down at him. His gaze seemed fixed on something just ahead of him. She felt a slight nudge of misgiving but ignored it. The little dog jumped up on her knee and gave a short, urgent bark. Celie hushed him. Toaster ignored her and barked again. A small bee buzzed past her ear.

Celie froze. For the first time, she saw a medium-sized brown box sitting on the ground just a few trees away from them. Her heart began to thump as she realized it was a beehive. Matthew had said to stay out of the west orchards today because they were pollinating the trees. She took a cautious step backward. Toaster started barking, so she picked him up. Another bee rumbled past.

Toaster squirmed so hard she almost dropped him. And then, suddenly, there were a lot of bees. She tried to wave them away and felt one sting her arm.

The sketchbook fell from her hand as she gripped Toaster, who was barking and snapping ferociously. She slapped the air, trying to protect them both. She spun around when a bee stung the back of her neck. She screamed. More bees were all around her now, blocking every direction.

"Celie," Matthew shouted. "Run!"

She glimpsed Matthew running toward her. Relief flooded her veins and gave strength to her legs. She ran toward him, clutching Toaster. The bees pursued, their awful droning filling her head.

She grabbed Matthew's hand, and together they raced through the grove of trees. The heel of her Jimmy Choo boot caught on a soft piece of earth. She almost fell, but Matthew steadied her just in time. Celie felt a pinch on her neck and another on her ear. Her lungs began to burn. Toaster felt as if he weighed a hundred pounds in her arms. When she tried to slow down, Matthew pulled her arm. The strength of his grip suggested her arm was coming out of the socket before the two of them stopped running.

It seemed like miles before the bees dropped back. And even then, Matthew barely let her slow down. They must have run another half mile before he allowed them to stop.

Celie set down Toaster and doubled over, breathing hard, dizzy, and slightly nauseous.

"Celie!" Matthew bent near her, grabbing her upper arms and peering anxiously into her face. "Celie! Are you allergic to bee stings? I need to know right now!"

Her brain wanted to answer, but her body couldn't seem to draw enough breath to form the words. He shook her urgently. "Are you allergic?" He was nearly shouting now, as if he thought the problem was her hearing. His face, mere inches from her own, was contorted with emotion.

"No." She gulped air and felt her stomach roll as if she had the flu. She concentrated on not throwing up on Matthew's brown work boots. He had huge feet, twice as big as hers. There was no way she could miss those feet if she got sick. She would have backed away, but he had a tight grip on her shoulders. "I'm fine," she panted. "Just give me a second."

He couldn't seem to do that, though. "Let me see the stings."

The stings didn't hurt as much as the stitch in her side, and she would assure him of this the minute she stopped gasping for breath. She lifted her face to let him see the damage was minor.

He snorted as if he were angry as he studied a sting just below her cheek. "Hold still," he ordered. "I'm going to get the stingers out before your skin starts to swell."

She braced herself as his fingers neared her. Like everything else about him, his hands were large. Her cheek tingled when he gently positioned his fingers around the stinger. Yesterday at the fabric store, his touch had been electric. She wasn't sure she could handle electricity right now.

"Hold still," he ordered gruffly. There was a small pinch on her cheek, then he said, "Got it." A small hesitation. "Did it hurt?"

"No," Celie said. "I hardly felt it."

"Good." His voice was gruff.

She watched his eyes as he took out the next one. Blue and serious, intent on their mission, the skin around them creased with concentration.

It felt strange to be eye level with him, nose to nose, their mouths level, eyes able to look straight into each other's. She'd never noticed how perfectly formed his lips were, softer, more full than she had thought. Another small pinch and a stinger seemed to pop miraculously into his hands.

There were five of them all together. "Any more?" His gaze searched her face.

She shook her head. "No." His eyebrows still had that pushed-together worried expression. "Matthew, I'm fine. Seriously, I've had worse accidents with sewing machines. When I was eleven, I actually sewed right through my thumbnail."

He made a face that suggested he'd rather not have known that, but he seemed to relax slightly. "In that case, would you mind telling me exactly what you were doing in the orchards when you knew I was pollinating the trees?"

"I heard you," Celie admitted softly. "But I wasn't going to go far—just sketch the apple trees near the house—and then Toaster got loose. When I finally caught up with him, there was this really great tree I wanted to draw." She watched his lips tighten and spoke a bit more rapidly. "The light on the leaves matched the colors of the fabrics we bought yesterday, and. . ."

"You risked getting hurt to sketch a tree?"

She looked away from the disbelief on his face. He thought she was an idiot. "Well, I didn't realize we'd gone so far." Celie decided she liked Matthew's worried face a lot more than this one. "And I didn't think we'd run into a swarm of bees, either. I figured there'd be some kind of warning sign. I'd hear them or see one or two, and I could turn around."

"It's not like New York City," Matthew said, frowning. "We don't have signs. You wandered too close to the hive. Toaster's barking probably made them feel threatened. That's why they attacked you."

"I'm sorry," she said, hoping to interrupt the safety lecture. She looked away from his eyes and focused on Toaster, who was in the process of eating grass. Poor thing was probably as unnerved about the whole bee thing as she was.

"This is the country."

"I know." Celie braced herself for some warning about getting eaten by wolves or getting lost and wandering for days in the orchards. He didn't say anything, though, and she turned back to him, confused.

"I heard you scream," he said gruffly. "And I knew right away it was you." He had a funny look in his eyes, and his mouth had a hard, set look. "You scared me."

Her hands shook as she brushed her bangs behind her ear. The way he was looking at her—it was like he really cared about her. "I'm sorry. Thank you, Matthew, for coming to my rescue."

"It's okay." His voice was matter-of-fact, the expression in his eyes frank. She wondered if she'd imagined there had been anything in his eyes moments before. He rose from the ground and did not offer to help her up. "Now let's go home."

ten

"Why don't we open up the windows, June? It's a beautiful morning." Celie crossed the living room to draw back the curtain and peer into the orchards. She had just finished helping June do her leg exercises, and the rest of the day stretched out in front of them.

"We don't have any screens in the windows," June replied and sighed with relief as she dropped into the velvet recliner. "Matthew took them out last fall when he winterized the house."

Through the glass, the May breeze moved through the vast orchards, bringing tree after tree to life. The wind chimes clanged lightly from the hook on the front porch. "We could put the screens back in the windows."

"Oh, but Matthew always does that."

"We could do it for him." Celie released the curtain and turned to face June.

"You'd have to take out the storm windows before you can put the screens in."

"I could do that," Celie said.

A slight flush remained high on June's cheeks, and a few wisps of silver hair floated free of her usual, neat bun—silent reminders of her morning exertion. "You're allowed as far as the mailbox, Celie, if you feel the need for fresh air, but remember, Matthew doesn't want you farther than that while they're pollinating the trees." She smiled. "How's the sewing coming on your dresses?"

"It's coming along fine—thanks to your Singer—but what about some fresh air? It smells so good outside, June. Like flowers."

"You can smell the buds, Celie? Everyone sees them, but

54

not everyone smells them." Her eyes held a trace of interest. "Kiera thought Matthew and I made that up, that we could smell the trees long before they produced any fruit."

Celie smiled. "You could be smelling those trees before the morning is over if you'll let me install the screens. We could make the whole house smell like roses."

June's mouth puckered as she considered Celie's words. She glanced at the windows and twisted her hands in her lap. "They're in the basement," she said at last, sounding as if she didn't care but sitting up a bit straighter. "Leaning up against the boxes with the Christmas decorations."

Celie retrieved the screens from a basement so crowded it was impossible to walk a straight line. She inched between stacked boxes, climbed over several old wooden sleds, and squeezed past an old Ping-Pong table holding a collection of pots, dishware, and an old pet carrier. There had to be at least twenty boxes of Christmas decorations, then she spotted the screens leaning against the sidewall, exactly where June said they would be.

"What's with all the boxes in the basement?" Celie asked as she walked into the living room and set the screens on the floor. She tied back the curtains and flung open the window. "I've never seen so many in my life."

"Oh, I never throw anything out," June said firmly. "It all comes in handy sooner or later."

The gutters in the windowsills needed cleaning, as did the metal tracks that held the screens. The windows themselves were dirty. June didn't have any Windex or Glass Plus, but she told Celie how to make a homemade cleaning solution out of ammonia, soapy water, and vinegar.

June supervised from her recliner at first but, seemingly unable to resist seeing Celie work, had begun following her from room to room, holding back the curtains as she lifted out the storm windows and installed the screens.

"Those storm windows are tricky things to install. Dermott, Matthew's father, always pinched his fingers on the levers. If that wasn't enough, I used to have a heart attack watching him leaning way out of the upstairs windows. He was such a big man, Celie. Hard for a man that size to have much grace, but he did." She paused. "He was a good man. Loved this family with every breath he had. One winter he duct-taped his boots together because we couldn't afford new ones. He bought the kids Flexible Flyer sleds for Christmas, though." She pointed with her finger. "You missed a spot there, honey."

Celie rubbed at the smudge on the glass. "I saw his picture on the wall. He and Matthew have the same eyes and jaw line."

"Yes," June agreed. "They do look alike. Matthew was only ten when he died." She paused. "Overnight he had to grow up. I would have had to sell this place if it weren't for him. Still would. Sometimes I wonder if it would have been better for him if I had."

Celie turned to meet June's gaze. "Matthew loves this farm. I can't imagine him being happy anywhere else."

"That's what I tell myself," June agreed. "But it's a lonely life here. For a while he was seeing Emily Taylor. Lovely girl. Her family has a horse farm a couple of miles from here. Raises Morgans. Most beautiful animals God ever created. Your eyes, Celie, are almost that same velvet brown as their coats." She paused as if to give Celie a moment to appreciate this compliment. "Emily used to pony a horse over here, and she and Matthew would ride for hours together in the orchards."

Celie fiercely scrubbed a minuscule smudge on the glass. "So what happened? Why didn't they get married?"

"Oh, she went to college and then graduate school and then got a writing job with the *Hartford Courant*. Life in the country wasn't her cup of tea."

Celie gazed out into the orchards. She imagined a teenage Matthew—all blue eyes and big-jointed bones—riding beside a beautiful blond girl named Emily. She pictured Emily saying something to Matthew, who would turn to her, laughing, his face open and beautiful.

The smudge was gone, but Celie kept rubbing. She wondered if Matthew still cared for this woman—if Emily Taylor was the reason he hadn't married or, for that matter, was not even dating.

A cool breeze moved through the installed screen, cooling cheeks Celie hadn't realized had grown so hot. Behind her, June inhaled deeply and sighed in pleasure. "Smell that, Celie? Only God's breath could be sweeter."

She smiled. "It's amazing. We should bottle it up and sell it." She moved to the next windowpane and swiped it with the ammonia mixture. The glass immediately went gray with the dissolving dirt and began to clear. Celie was less successful in eliminating the image of Emily Taylor from her mind.

❧

By lunchtime they'd finished installing all the screens in the downstairs windows. Celie heated a can of tomato soup and made grilled cheese sandwiches. As the food heated on the stove, she wondered about Matthew—silly things, like his favorite flavor of ice cream and what color he liked best. What had his childhood been like? And of course, she was consumed with curiosity about anything and everything involving Emily Taylor.

She set a plate down in front of June. "Here you go. I made an extra in case Matthew decided to join us."

June tore off the corner and slipped it to Toaster. "Oh, I doubt we'll see him for lunch until after the bees finish pollinating the orchards." She gave Celie a sly look. "Of course, he may come home early and check on you. He asked me three times when you were out of earshot to keep an eye on you."

"I don't need anyone keeping an eye on me."

June's voice was gentle. "Everyone needs someone looking out for them."

After lunch Celie suggested the windows would look even better if they washed the curtains. June resisted. "Those old drapes are so old they'll fall apart."

"If they do," Celie assured her, "I know someone who can fix them."

Standing on a kitchen chair and reaching up with every inch of her five-foot-one frame, Celie unhooked the cotton panels and brought them down to the basement to wash. While the curtains dried, Celie vacuumed. After that was finished, June glanced around. "Feels so much fresher in here. Now if we could only make the furniture look less tired."

Celie liked the sparkle in June's eye. "The mirror in the dining room would look great on the mantel, and the portrait of Great-Grandma Caroline could hang in the dining room."

June cocked her head uncertainly. "The mirror's heavy, Celie. I'm not sure a regular picture hook will hold it."

"We aren't going to hang it, exactly. I'll show you."

❧

Celie was upstairs, getting changed, when she heard Matthew come through the back door. There was no mistaking the thump of the door or Toaster's howl of pleasure. She checked the back of her earrings. The house looked beautiful, and she wanted to look her best as well. She'd decided her pencil skirt and ruffled blouse would be festive choices.

She hurried down the stairs and into the living room. Matthew stood with his back to her, hands on his hips, staring at the mirror on the mantelpiece. She couldn't wait to see his reaction. "You like it?"

Matthew spun around. "What did you do?"

Celie drew back at the coldness in his voice. "We cleaned the curtains and moved a few things around."

"I can see that."

If Matthew's jaw got any tighter, it was going to take surgery to loosen it. She couldn't understand. The room looked great, and the air smelled fresh and clean.

"You don't like it." Behind her bafflement, Celie felt the sharp edges of disappointment.

"It was fine the way it was," Matthew said. "What did you do with Great-Grandmother Caroline's portrait?"

"In the dining room." Where it belonged. If he would only look, he would see that.

"I don't think it's safe for a heavy mirror like that just to be leaning against a mantel." Matthew crossed the room in three strides and tested the mirror's stability. He looked even less pleased when it didn't budge. "Where's the Log Cabin quilt?" he said abruptly. "The one that hangs on the back of the sofa?"

"Upstairs," Celie replied. "I'm going to sew a backing and get a wooden hanger. It'll look great on that big wall over there."

She gestured to the wall flanking the steep staircase, but Matthew's gaze didn't falter from her face. "The quilt belongs on the back of the sofa."

"Matthew Patrick." June thumped into the room behind her walker. "I heard you clearly from the kitchen. That is no way to talk to a guest in our home. You will apologize to Celie immediately. She's worked hard all day to bring a little beauty into our home and doesn't deserve to bear the brunt of your foul humor."

Matthew's eyebrows pushed together. "Our house was beautiful enough."

"I wasn't saying your house wasn't beautiful," Celie said, trying hard to keep her temper. How could this be the same man who had so gently removed her bee stings? "All I was trying to do was bring more light into the room."

"We don't need any more light in here. Put everything back. In fact, I'll help you right now."

As he reached for the mirror on the mantelpiece, however, the front doorbell rang. Matthew froze, a quizzical expression replacing the look of annoyance. He turned to June, who looked equally surprised. Then a hopeful smile appeared on her face. "You think it's Kiera?"

eleven

Toaster beat him to the door, barking and showing every sign of making a run for it the minute an opening appeared. Matthew scooped the excited dog into his arms. "Stop yapping," he told the squirming Toaster.

He pulled open the door. His neighbor, Jeremy Taylor, stood on the porch. Jeremy was a tall, thin man with white hair as thick as a lion's mane. He was in his seventies, and yet the handshake he gave Matthew was firmer and stronger than men's half his age.

"Jeremy," Matthew said, smiling. "Come inside. It's good to see you."

"You, too, Matthew," Jeremy said, following him into the foyer. "Sorry to stop by without calling."

"You don't have to call," Matthew assured him.

"You never need to call," June echoed as Matthew led Jeremy into the living room. "You're always welcome here. Can I get you something to drink? Coffee?"

Jeremy smiled but shook his head. "I won't stay but a moment." His gaze moved from June to Celie, who stood wearing that frothy-looking shirt, the slender skirt, and those high-heeled boots. Matthew frowned, but mainly at himself. He didn't want to feel attracted to her, but he did.

"You remember Celie Donovan," Matthew said, remembering his manners. "Kiera's friend?"

Jeremy smiled. "Of course. We spoke at church last week. It's nice to see you again."

"You, too," Celie said, smiling her usual, warm smile. Matthew could see Jeremy visibly brightening in response.

"How's Emily?" his mother asked. "We were just talking

about her this afternoon, Celie and I. We were doing some spring-cleaning."

"Oh, she's doing fine," Jeremy said. "Working too many hours, as usual. We keep up, though. On the computer. Never imagined that instant messaging would replace a phone call, but that's the way it is with young people these days."

"Maybe for you," June replied, "but I will never use the computer for anything. I leave all that technical mumbo-jumbo stuff to Matthew."

The gazes turned to him. "Well, tell Emily I said hi and not to neglect the country," Matthew said, smiling, although it had not always been easy to hear Emily's name and smile.

"The reason I'm here," Jeremy said, fishing in the pocket of his coat, "is to bring you this. It came to my mailbox by mistake. Got caught in a magazine."

Jeremy handed his mother a colorful postcard. Matthew glimpsed the flash of a beach scene. His mother's face went white, and she all but snatched it from the older man's hands. She turned over the back and eagerly scanned the contents.

Matthew lifted the card from his mother's shaking hands. It was from his sister.

Hola, Mom and Matthew, he read. *The cruise was amazing! Now I'm in Mexico. It's beautiful! I miss you all but am having fun. More later, and love, Kiera.*

Noticeably absent were Kiera's plans to return to Connecticut. Matthew returned the card to his mother and hid his disgust in what he hoped was a neutral expression.

"Well, at least we know she's alive and kicking," his mother said calmly, passing the card to Celie who read it and glanced at him as if he could explain what in the world was going on with his sister.

"Thank you so much for bringing this over, Jeremy," his mom continued. "We've been worried. Kiera's in Mexico—on an extended vacation—and this is the first word from her."

Jeremy studied his mother's face. "Is everything okay, June?"

She sighed. "Yeah, I think so. Kiera needed a little time to herself. That awful man from the city dumped her, and she needed to get away for a while." She gave him a small smile. "Kids. They never grow so old that you stop worrying about them. You'll stay for supper, won't you? Celie made a roast, and there's plenty of it."

"It smells delicious," Jeremy said. "Nothing an old widower likes more than a home-cooked meal. But I don't want to impose. June, while I'm here, I wanted to talk to you about this year's rummage sale at the church. I raised my hand at the wrong time and ended up being the chairperson of the event."

"Oh Jeremy, why didn't you simply unvolunteer yourself?" his mother asked.

"I tried, but all the ladies in the room thought it would be great to have a man's perspective." He shrugged unhappily. "I told them I don't know a thing about clothing, but they said it was more a matter of organizing things than anything else. By the time they'd finished, Rev. Westover said he'd take it as a personal favor if I would lead this event."

"You're too nice for your own good." June stroked Toaster, who had jumped into her lap.

"Well, like it or not, I'm the chairperson." He paused. "I was hoping you'd be my cochair." He paused again. "I'm already getting boxes of donations, and I don't know what to do with them."

"Me?" His mother's silver eyebrows lifted. "I'm flattered you would think of me. But Jeremy, my hip really slows me down these days. I rarely leave the house."

"I'm slowing down, too. However, the Lord made rabbits and He made turtles and He uses them both." Jeremy laughed. He had an easy way about him that Matthew had always admired. After his dad passed away, Jeremy had put his hand on Matthew's shoulder, looked deeply into his eyes, and promised to be there if Matthew ever needed him. "I won't try to take your dad's place," he'd explained, "but I'm here for you as a friend." Matthew had never taken him up on it, but there had been times in his life when he thought long and hard about doing it. It'd always seemed a bit disloyal to his dad.

"I don't know, Jeremy," June said doubtfully. "It's a lot of work."

That was the understatement of the century. Matthew ran his hand through his hair. The rummage sale traditionally was a disaster. People enthusiastically emptied their closets, but nobody really bought much. Last year he'd transported an entire truckload of unwanted clothing to the Salvation Army.

"I'll bring everything to you. You wouldn't even have to leave the house."

"I could help, too," Celie commented. "We could get some garment racks, June. You and I could sort and tag the clothes, and then Matthew could return the racks to the church. It'd be fun."

Matthew's gaze shot to Celie's face. He mouthed *no* and shook his head. Celie had no idea. This wasn't just a few boxes of donations. It was mountains of clothing. He wasn't sure June could handle the amount of work required. His gaze narrowed. Was Celie volunteering his mother just to extend her stay?

"Why don't you ask Susan Grojack?" June suggested. "Didn't she lead this last year?"

"She's taken a secretarial job with the town."

"Oh," his mother said, her lips puckering. "I didn't know."

"We could do this," Celie said. "It'd be fun, June."

"You have your own sewing to do." His mother looked at Jeremy. "Celie's a marvelous designer."

"Aspiring designer," Celie corrected. "Currently unemployed and available. This rummage sale sounds like a good cause." She shot Matthew a significant look. "I'm sure June's friends at the church would be glad to come over and help, too."

"Of course they would," Jeremy said.

His mother rubbed her left hip as if it had suddenly started to ache and shot Matthew a mute appeal for help.

He frowned. His mom had been on one church committee or another practically her whole life. Declining this opportunity seemed to be one more example of his mother's giving up, reducing her world to nothing more than the four walls around her.

He glanced back at Celie and suddenly understood. Her intention wasn't to prolong her stay but to bring more action and a purpose into his mother's life. He felt stupid for not seeing this earlier. "You should do it," Matthew urged. "Celie's right. It's a good cause."

June's mouth opened. She looked from his face to Celie's and then back to his again as if searching for an excuse and not finding one.

"If it gets to be too much work for you, I promise to get someone else," Jeremy offered.

His mom wrung her hands and glanced once more at Matthew, who smiled encouragement. "I guess I could give it a try."

"We'll have fun," Celie promised.

"The last time she said that," his mother said in a deadpan, "I ended up flat on my back doing leg lifts."

"This will be easier than leg lifts," Jeremy said, laughing. "I'll start dropping boxes off tomorrow, whenever it's convenient."

"Anytime's good, Jeremy." His mom's cheeks pinked up a bit. "Why don't you come for lunch?"

"I'd love to." Standing, he thanked everyone and said it was time for him to go. Pausing beneath the archway, he looked back, his eyebrows bunched together. "Did you change something in here?" He glanced around. "The room looks bigger than I remember. Brighter, too. I like it."

The two women exchanged smiles. With a sinking feeling, Matthew realized the furniture arrangement was going to stay.

twelve

The next morning, Celie found her sketchbook lying on the braided rug outside her bedroom door. With a small exclamation of surprised joy, she flipped it open. The pages were slightly curled, the cardboard backing damp, but her sketches were completely intact.

The last time she'd seen this book was when she'd been swatting bees and trying to hold on to Toaster. Matthew had gone back for it. There was no other explanation. She clutched the book to her chest and hurried down the stairs.

June sat at the kitchen table sipping a cup of tea, Toaster firmly ensconced in her lap. Instead of the sweat suits Celie had grown used to seeing her wear, she'd dressed in jeans and a green wool cardigan. "Morning, Celie."

"You look nice, June." She gazed from June to the empty place setting at the head of the table.

"You just missed him," June commented, following her glance. "He went up to the barn."

"Oh." It was barely six thirty in the morning. Matthew usually didn't leave until seven. She glanced at the half-empty pot of coffee and the bacon drying on its bed of paper towels. Her gaze lingered on a ceramic mug with a tea bag hanging over the side. He'd made her tea.

"Is there anything I can do, dear?"

Celie shook her head. "He found my sketchbook." She held out the wire-bound spiral as if in explanation. "I wanted to thank him."

"Why don't you run up to the barn? I'm sure you can catch him before he heads into the orchards." June smiled. "Take Toastie with you. He loves going up to the barn, don't you, little Toastie?" She patted the dog's tufted head. "Go on now."

Toaster bounced about her, pulling at the boundaries imposed by his leash as they stepped into the cold May morning. Celie pulled the belt of her trench tighter.

She found Matthew outside the barn's oversized front door. He was emptying plastic water buckets into the grass. Picking up the pace, she pulled Toaster away from an interesting scent and reached Matthew just as he was emptying the last bucket. "Missed you at breakfast."

Matthew straightened. "Is everything okay?" He looked back at the house.

"Everything is fine." Even in her heels, she hardly reached Matthew's shoulder. "I just wanted to thank you for finding my sketchbook."

He shrugged, picked up a spray hose lying nearby, and began to rinse out the buckets. "You're welcome. Thanks for encouraging my mom to take on the rummage sale."

"Oh yeah, well, I figured she could use a project. You didn't get stung or anything, did you?" She scanned him for injury. It was hard to tell with his head bent and a thick chamois shirt covering his upper body, but he seemed okay.

He looked up then, and she read something in his eyes. "You got stung, didn't you? Oh, Matthew. I would never have let you go back for the sketchbook."

"Let's just leave it at thank-you," Matthew said, carrying the buckets back into the barn. "It wasn't a big deal."

"It was a big deal. It has some sketches I need." She followed him into the dimly lit barn, stopping short as he entered the stall of the enormous brown horse. Tall as Matthew was, his head just barely came up to the horse's shoulder. He clipped the water buckets back in place.

"You'd better step back," Matthew warned. "I'm going to take Bonnie out of her stall."

Celie retreated to the other side of the barn as Bonnie slowly clomped into the aisle. Outside her stall, she seemed even bigger, with huge hindquarters and rippling muscles. The shaggy hair on the bottom of Bonnie's legs reminded

Celie of a dress she'd once designed out of feathers.

She twisted her fingers together, reminding herself that Matthew had risked injury to get her sketchbook and she ought to do something to thank him. "You want some help?"

Pitchfork in hand, he looked at her over the top of the waist-high stall door. "What?"

"You want some help?" Celie repeated, this time a bit more loudly. She tightened her grip on Toaster's leash, who was trying to lick something awful off the concrete floor.

"No," he said.

"You sure?" The goats bleated from their stall, and Celie nearly jumped a foot. "I could help you clean."

His dark eyebrows lifted. "You? Clean a stall?"

Celie squared her shoulders. "Yes, me."

He laughed. "No thanks."

"Oh. Well. I could sweep the aisle or dust or. . ." She looked around trying to come up with another chore a person might do at a barn. "Matthew, those sketches meant a lot to me. I'd really like to help you."

He seemed to think about this a bit. "Bonnie could use some grooming."

Celie gazed at the horse standing placidly in the aisle. She looked harmless. But she was awfully big. Celie wasn't sure what he meant by groom her.

"The brushes are right in that tack trunk over there."

Celie brightened. Brushes. He meant make the horse look pretty. Bonnie's mane did look a bit tangled, and there were bits of white shavings clinging to her coat. She tied Toaster's leash to a ring on the wall and went to work.

&

"So how, exactly, are you going to get your old boss to look at your green dress when it's finished?" Matthew turned over a pitchfork of bedding and separated the clean from the soiled. "Since they fired you, I doubt you're going to be allowed back in the building."

"Good point," Celie replied. "I'll have to talk to James about that. He's really smart. And he got really mad when they fired me. He'll help."

Matthew stopped with the pitchfork in midair. Just who was James? Her boyfriend? He digested the possibility slowly and didn't like the way it sat with him. It was none of his business, but he heard himself ask, "James is another designer?"

"No." She laughed. "James is in accounting. He works in the executive suites, but he spends a lot of time talking to us in the workroom. We kept having to hide him from Libby Ellman—she's the head designer. Libby's always checking up on everybody."

One of the things Matthew liked best about working on the orchards was the freedom to control his day. He couldn't imagine working in an environment where someone was constantly looking over his shoulder.

"This one time, Libby went on the warpath looking for James because he signed off on too much overtime for the hourly employees. He ran into the workroom with Libby hard on his heels, and we disguised him as a mannequin." Celie giggled happily. "A girl mannequin! We padded him up, strategically draped fabric around him, and put a hat on him. Libby walked right past him! We laughed so hard we almost cried."

She laughed, and the sound filled the barn. Matthew found himself laughing, too. She told him other funny stories, and all too soon Matthew finished cleaning the stall. He pushed the wheelbarrow into the aisle, stopping short when he saw Bonnie. "What in the world did you do to her?"

Celie beamed down at him from atop a bale of hay. "I groomed her."

He pointed to the mare's head. "She's wearing a hat and sunglasses."

"I know. Doesn't she look nice?"

Bonnie's ears stuck through the top of a floppy straw hat that had once graced the head of a homemade scarecrow. For years the straw man had guarded June's vegetable garden.

But then the garden had become too much work, and they'd stored the scarecrow in the corner of the barn. Unfortunately, the goats had gotten loose a couple of times and eaten most of the scarecrow, including part of the hat. He wasn't sure where she'd found the sunglasses.

"I thought you were going to groom her, not deck her out like she's going to a garden party."

"You said groom her, and that's exactly what I'm doing." Celie smiled down at him from her perch. Her fingers twisted Bonnie's mane into small braids.

"I meant get the dirt off her."

"She likes the hat, Matthew. It makes her feel pretty."

"Horses don't feel pretty—or ugly or fat or skinny, either."

"That's nonsense," Celie said. "Everyone feels better about themselves if they feel attractive. The minute Bonnie saw that hat, she put her head right down so I could put it over her ears."

"If she lowered her head," Matthew argued, enjoying himself tremendously, "it was because she thought it was something to eat." He had to bite the inside of his cheek to keep from laughing.

He moved closer to Celie. On the bale of hay, she stood just a little taller than him. Matthew had to look up to meet her gaze. He found this new perspective very intriguing. He could lift her right off that bale with one arm if he wanted to. To his dismay, he discovered he very much wanted to.

He reached for the mare's hat instead. Celie's cry stopped him. "I think June should see Bonnie before you undress her."

"She won't come up," he said gruffly. "Not anymore."

"Why not?" The words were said gently, but they still stung. "Why won't she come up to the barn anymore, Matthew?"

He shook his head, the last bit of Celie's laughter fading from his mind. "I don't know. For a while I thought she was scared of falling again, but now I don't think that's it at all."

"What happened?" Her voice was velvety soft. "How did she break her hip?"

The familiar guilt rose like a wave over him. For a moment he couldn't speak, could only remember walking through the house, taking his time to eat a peach over the sink, and having no idea that his mother was flat at the bottom of the hayloft steps, unable to even crawl for help.

"She slipped on those steps and fell," he said, pointing to the open staircase leading to the loft. "It was two hours before I found her. I should never have allowed her to throw down bales of hay. What was I thinking, allowing a seventy-year-old woman to do something like that?"

It didn't matter that right until that point his mother had been striding around the farm, ordering people around, and hefting fifty-pound sacks of feed over her shoulder. He should have seen her growing more fragile. He should have seen some sign of her aging.

He felt a light touch on his arm. Celie was looking down at him with an expression of deep sympathy in her velvet brown eyes. "It wasn't your fault."

"Of course it's my fault. I should have looked after her better." His gaze hardened. "I should have looked after Kiera better, too." Why was he confiding things to Celie he had never admitted to anyone else before?

He wanted to reach for her. He knew if he let himself, he'd kiss her. And that wasn't a very good idea at all. *Why her, God? Why do I have to like this woman? Why couldn't I feel this way about Bekka Johnson?* Bekka was pretty, loved children, and sang in the church choir. She would never put a straw hat on a horse if he'd asked her to groom it. And she never would have moved all the furniture around or nearly wandered into a beehive.

And maybe that's why he'd felt nothing for Bekka. He couldn't remember her making him laugh, either.

He set his jaw, more aware than ever of Celie so close.

Please Lord, not her.

Matthew pulled the straw hat from the mare's head and tossed it into a corner. Bonnie lifted her massive head, startled by the abruptness of his gesture. He felt Celie's gaze on his back but did not let himself look at her face as he led the big horse back to her stall.

thirteen

Celie helped June make a salad and spinach quiche for lunch. As she whisked the eggs and cheese together, she kept thinking about Matthew—the frustration on his face, the pain in his voice. It wasn't his fault June had fallen, and it wasn't his fault Kiera had run off to Mexico, either. Sometimes bad things happened. You simply had to live with them and trust God to use them for His purpose. It pained her to think of Matthew living with guilt.

June sat at the kitchen table, tearing lettuce into a pretty glass bowl with hand-painted flowers. "You think spinach quiche is too feminine a meal for Jeremy? You think we should have made cheeseburgers?"

"He'll love the quiche," Celie assured her. "And if he doesn't, he can always fill up on the blueberry pie and ice cream."

"That's true," June agreed. "You think we have time to bake some rolls?"

Celie hid a smile. She had a feeling June would keep adding to the menu until Jeremy walked through the door. She just hoped Jeremy came hungry.

Soon the house was filled with the delicious aroma of baking quiche. Celie was testing the quiche for doneness—it needed a few more minutes—when she heard the front door open. She was just in time to watch Matthew and Jeremy walk through the hallway, their arms full of large cardboard boxes.

"Where do you want them?" Jeremy asked.

June looked at Celie. "I don't know."

"How many are there?" Celie asked.

"Ten," Matthew said.

"Oh my," June said. "That many already?"

72

"The ladies dropped off a few more at the church today," Jeremy admitted, shifting his weight, "and there are more coming in every day."

"Why don't we put them in the dining room?" Celie suggested.

June brightened. "Perfect."

As Matthew and Jeremy brought in more boxes, Celie and June opened the first two. June pulled out a pair of light blue jeans. The denim had worn through at the knees, and it looked as if someone had taken a pair of pinking shears to the ends of both legs. "We should just throw those away," June said, casting them aside to search the rest of the box.

Celie took the jeans. The material above the knee wasn't bad. The rise was a little high, but with a little alteration, she could turn the jeans into Bermuda shorts. She laid the denim aside and pulled out a crumpled yellow dress.

June made a face at the garment in Celie's hands. "That's just plain ugly. The only use for that would be if someone wanted material for a tent."

Matthew and Jeremy returned with another stack of boxes. They stopped dead in their tracks when they saw Celie holding up the yellow dress.

"Why did someone donate a yellow tablecloth?" Matthew asked.

"It's a dress," Celie said. "And with a little work, it could be pretty. You just add some ruching here and add a waistband—an empire waist would work well, I think, and some trim."

"What's ruche?" Jeremy continued to study the dress with an expression of horrified fascination.

"It's a term for gathering."

"You could gather that dress from one end to another, and it'd still be a sow's ear." June cast aside a patchwork skirt. "It's like the rest of what's in this box. All the sewing in the world can't turn these garments into silk purses."

"Maybe we should have lunch," Matthew suggested. "Something smells good."

Celie pulled a pair of black wool slacks out of another box. "The cut of the leg is wrong, but they have a beautiful lining." She turned the fabric inside out to demonstrate. "I could turn these pants into a pencil skirt. I'd put a slit in the back, so the lining could peek through. We could pair it with this blouse." Celie held up a black-and-white patterned shirt.

"It's very nice," Jeremy said, but he sounded unsure.

June laughed. "What woman wants to dress up in zebra stripes?"

"Lots of women," Celie promised. "Animal prints are fashionable right now. Besides, this shirt has great seaming. We might add a pop of color somewhere—a red purse maybe—or red high heels. But an outfit like this one would sell for a lot of money in New York City."

"Well, I guess so. If anyone knows fashion, it's you." June turned to Jeremy and said, "If her designs hadn't gotten burned up, they would have been showcased in a very important fashion show in New York City."

Celie already had her hands around a velvet jacket. She liked the poufed shoulders—but the mutton-shaped arms had to go. She'd turn the jacket into a vest. *Hold on a second*, a small voice inside her said. *Do you really want to get so heavily involved with this project? The more time you spend on these clothes, the less time you'll have for sewing your own dress—and the longer you'll be staying on this farm.* She thought of all the sacrifices her parents had made so she could attend the Rhode Island School of Design, of all the hours she and her mother had spent dreaming about the day when Celie's dresses would hang in the windows of stores like Saks Fifth Avenue and appear in the pages of magazines like *Harper's Bazaar.*

She fingered the velvet. Maybe, like June had said, she was exactly where God wanted her to be. *Do You want me to do this?* She wasn't completely sure, but it felt right. "It wouldn't take me long to put together some outfits you could showcase at the sale. It might inspire people to look at the rest of the clothing a little differently."

"And maybe buy things," Jeremy stroked his chin. "You know what would be even better?"

"Lunch?" Matthew suggested hopefully.

"If we could get some volunteers from the church to wear the clothes Celie alters." Jeremy ran his hands through his thick cloud of white hair.

"You mean model them?" June looked excited.

"Exactly," Jeremy said. "When we want to sell a horse, we take it out of the stall and put it through its paces. My guess is that if you want to sell clothing, you have to show how great someone can look wearing it."

Celie put the velvet down and stared at Jeremy. "You're talking a fashion show, aren't you?"

Jeremy nodded.

"We could call it 'Castoffs to Couture,'" Celie suggested, already picturing the event. "That way it'd suggest original designs but also let people know the clothing isn't new."

"Every woman in town would want to come. It could be a huge fund-raiser for the church." June turned eagerly to Celie. "You could invite your boss and then dazzle him with your designs."

Hmmm. She hadn't considered that aspect. Would Mr. Marcus laugh at a small-town church fashion show—or would he see that he'd made a huge mistake letting her go?

"Hold on, Mom," Matthew said. "I think we're getting a little ahead of ourselves here. A fashion show is a lot of work. And besides, aren't you forgetting something?"

June's lips puckered. "Like what?"

"Like you should talk to Rev. Westover and the rest of the church elders before you completely reinvent the rummage sale."

"I don't think that would be a problem," Jeremy said slowly. "The numbers from last year's rummage sale really weren't that good. I think that's why everyone was so quick to draft me into the chairperson role in the first place. I'll talk to the reverend in the morning, but I don't see anyone objecting to this change." His gaze softened as he looked at June. "And I'll make sure we get extra help."

"That'd be great, Jeremy," Celie said. "I could really use some dress dummies—as many different sizes as possible. And I'll need a worktable, sewing machines, lots of sewing notions, ironing board and iron. And racks for hanging the clothing." She wrinkled her brow. "If anyone can sew, that'd be a help, too. Oh, and a mirror. As big as possible."

"I've got an old dress dummy and a standing mirror, too." June turned to Matthew. "Could you please bring them down?"

❧

Matthew started up the old, wooden stairs. A fashion show? A burst of laughter followed him up. He reached the second-floor landing and started up the third flight of stairs. He didn't want to picture half the ladies in town trying to wear the same kind of formfitting skirts and frothy white shirts as Celie wore. The town had absolutely no idea what it might be getting into, not one small bit.

The attic boards creaked under his feet. The wind stirred the cold air in the rafters. This high up, he could see for miles out the dusty window—cold storage barns, the rows of trees budding, ready for the seedlings that would form and grow. Change was coming to the orchard, as it did every season. This was a good thing, a God thing. He understood this. Gave thanks for this.

The changes in the house, the stirrings in his own heart— these things felt uncomfortable to him, unsettling and vaguely threatening. He'd started having trouble sleeping, too, catching only a few hours at a time. When he woke, he couldn't remember his dreams, only that they had been vivid and sweet and that Celie's name was on his lips.

Matthew tucked the sewing dummy under his arm and headed down the steps. He prayed that God would give him guidance.

fourteen

"Is this too tight?" June pulled the back seams of the muslin fabric tightly together.

"As long as I don't breathe," Celie said, feeling as if her ribs were touching. The pressure on her rib cage eased a bit. "Thank you." She gave a sigh of relief.

"I think it should be tight," June said unapologetically. "You need to show off that tiny waist."

"It's not that tiny," Celie stated. "And the way I'm eating, it's getting less tiny every day."

They stood in the dining room, curtains drawn for privacy, and gazed at each other from the image within the frame of an antique standing mirror.

"You think it looks right?" With all the sewing work she had, it had taken Celie more than a week to translate the drawings from her sketchbook into a pattern and then several more evenings to cut the pieces and baste them together.

"Yes. And it'll look even better," June observed dryly from behind her, "without Kiera's old ballet leotard and tights on underneath."

Celie laughed. She shifted to catch another angle. The bodice fit well—she didn't see any major changes she needed to make. But this was just a test garment, sewn from inexpensive muslin.

She tugged the bodice a fraction higher, imagining the way she'd weave together strips of green and yellow silk for the bodice and the way the silk would spill to the floor. It would look completely natural but would take hours of carefully placing darts. Lifting herself onto her toes, she pictured someone tall and elegant-looking wearing the finished dress. Someone taller, less curvy than herself. Someone like Kiera.

She felt a quick pang of anxiety and a longing to talk to her best friend, gone now almost a month and not a word since that postcard two weeks ago.

June met her gaze in the mirror's reflection. "Poor Matthew. When this dress is finished and he sees you in it, he isn't going to have a chance." She tsked happily. "Poor, poor Matthew."

Celie rolled her eyes. "It isn't like that with us, June." She turned away from the mirror, unable to define just what her relationship was with Matthew. They weren't friends, and they weren't enemies. They were sort of like oil and water. Two liquids that wouldn't blend together unless forced to.

"It's exactly like that," June said but more gently this time.

Celie pretended to study the side seam very closely. Matthew had seemed to be in a better mood these past couple of days, but she felt sure the change had everything to do with the progress June's hip continued to make. She'd stopped using the walker and now relied on a glossy black cane. And occasionally she didn't even need that.

The telephone rang. Ever since Jeremy had gotten the church to agree to the fashion show, the phone had been ringing off the hook. "Shoot me dead the next time I volunteer for something," June said, but Celie noticed a certain eagerness in her step as she headed for the kitchen.

Celie could hear June's voice as she changed into a pair of jeans, layered a couple of T-shirts, and slipped on her battle-scarred, but still lovely, Jimmy Choo boots.

"Claire is either giving me measurements prior to child-birth or else she's had one too many cups of herbal tea," June commented, returning to the room. "She wants to model swimwear. I told her we wanted to sell clothing, not make people cover their eyes."

Laughing, Celie picked up a brown blazer and began opening up the seams. "I heard you clearly, June. You told her you'd put her down for swimwear, if there were any."

June walked slowly over to Celie, the glossy black cane thumping on the hardwood floor. "I know. I couldn't think of anything else to say. I guess you'd better be generous in your sizing, Celie. Half the women who've volunteered to model are subtracting inches off their hips."

The two women exchanged smiles. "We'll have a fitting prior to the show. Everything will be fine."

"If anyone should be modeling swimwear, it's Kiera," June mused. "She was always beautiful from the day she was born. Difficult, though. Screamed her head off as a baby and had that awful reflux—threw up over *everything*. Not like Matthew. He was always smiling, always content in himself."

Matthew—a happy baby? It was hard to reconcile this image with the strong, serious man he had become.

"Dermott loved both his kids," June continued, pulling up a chair next to Celie. "But Matthew was his favorite. Dermott used to sit him on top of his shoulders and take him out into the orchards. Before he could walk, Dermott had introduced him to every tree on the farm. 'I want him to love three things,' Dermott always said. 'The Lord first and foremost, then his family, and of course, the land.'"

She picked up a pincushion from the table and absently began rearranging the pins. "I wish Dermott had been able to instill the same love of the land in Kiera. Maybe he would have, if he'd had more time. Maybe I should have done things differently. God knows I did the best I could."

Celie touched June's arm. "She loves you. She'll be back. You just have to hang in a little longer."

June nodded. "I know it, but some days I feel about as strong as a limp noodle."

"I understand," Celie said. "I've felt like that, too. You just have to trust that God will work things out. Like you told me, you have to keep trying, keep believing, no matter what." She slipped her arm around the older woman and pulled her against her side.

"What if something bad has happened to her?" June's voice was hardly a whisper. "I couldn't stand it."

Celie's arm tightened. How thin June's bones felt, how very

breakable. Celie wanted to take her in her arms and hold her, love her as if she were her own mother. At the same time, June sat with her back ramrod straight, as if some small part of her refused to succumb to the weight of the fears inside her.

"I'm sorry," June said at last. "Usually I try not to burden anyone with my own fears." She shook her head. "I know Kiera is a grown woman, but in some ways, she's so fragile. Losing her father so young. . ." She paused. "In some ways, I think she's still missing him, looking to fill that void he left."

"She may have lost her father," Celie said gently, "but she knows she has a heavenly Father who will never leave her. Did she ever tell you that she and I used to meet for services at Saint Patrick's Cathedral?"

June glanced up, relief in her large blue eyes. "It helps to hear that, Celie. It helps to see you living your faith. I know you lost everything in that fire. Yet I've never heard you complain."

Celie smiled. "Trust me. God and I have had a lot of talks."

In the distance, the sound of a car drifted into the room. "Is that Jeremy already?" June asked.

Celie rose to her feet to peer out the window. Light flooded the room as she pulled back the curtain, and she saw the familiar colors of the U.S. Postal truck. "Not Jeremy, but the mail's here. I'll take Toaster and go bring it in."

fifteen

Jeremy's car wasn't parked in the driveway, and when Matthew opened the back door, the house seemed much quieter than usual. He found Celie in the kitchen, stirring something in a big pot on the cooktop. "Hey," he said in greeting. "I didn't see Jeremy's car. He leave already?"

She turned around, her expression tense. "He didn't come today. June asked him not to."

He frowned. "Why? Where is she, anyway?"

"In her chair. Resting." Celie crossed the room and picked a card off the kitchen table. "This came today."

The postcard showed a picture of a red-hued sunset over the water and a man and a woman taking a romantic walk on the beach. His pulse picked up. Kiera. He flipped the card over.

Hola, Mom and Matthew!
   The best news ever. I met a nice guy. His name is Benji Bateman, and he's the ship's photographer. We're staying in Cozumel at this beautiful old villa. My room has a beautiful view of the water, but poor Benji has to sleep in the basement. The señora here is very strict—but that's okay. Both Benji and I want to get things exactly right this time. I really think he's special. Please don't worry about me.
                                          I love you both,
                                                  Kiera

He clenched his jaw and resisted the urge to rip the postcard into a thousand pieces. What was she thinking? Running straight from one man into the arms of another? And a ship's photographer? *The ship's* unemployed *photographer*, he corrected himself.

"I'm going down there and bringing her back," Matthew said. "She's obviously lost her mind."

"You can't do that," his mother said from the doorway. She looked awful, her face devoid of color and the lines deeper than he had ever seen them. "You make her come back here, and she'll just run away again. She's a grown woman, able to make her own choices."

"She can make her own choices when she starts making good ones," Matthew stated, wondering what papers he needed for a passport and how much time it would take.

"Maybe you should just give her a little more time," Celie suggested. "If we don't hear from her in a week or so, then look into going down there."

"Wait? When she's obviously in a fragile emotional state?" Matthew glared at Celie—the woman who'd tripped the first domino in this mess that had become his sister's life. "I'm supposed to sit around and let some guy who probably sees that she's vulnerable take advantage of her? Isn't Bateman the name of the guy in *Psycho*?"

"That was Bates. And I don't think you have a choice," Celie said. "Even if you had a passport, it's not like you have an address or a phone number. How are you going to find them?"

"Celie's right," his mom said. "You have to let this be, Matthew. At least for now. She's in God's hands now." She exchanged glances with Celie.

Although part of Matthew registered that this might be true, he also couldn't help but feel that he was responsible for his sister's welfare. You didn't promise your dying father that you'd look after everyone and then forget about it just because you didn't have a passport.

His mind raced. There had to be a multitude of villas, but maybe the ship's captain would have an idea where his ship's photographer might have gone. But he could do all these things, he realized, and Celie and his mother could be right. Kiera could flatly refuse to come home.

"I'm going out." He grabbed his Windbreaker from a peg in the mudroom. The door shut with a satisfyingly loud bang behind him. He walked quickly, taking deep breaths of cold air and trying to calm down. He glanced up at the silver stars.

Heavenly Father, why is she doing this? How can she possibly think some womanizer from the ship is special? How can she be so naive? Please open her eyes to the truth.

His thoughts led him to the wooden shed discreetly tucked to the side of the house. The small building housed his four-wheeler, tools, and worktable. Growing up, he'd spent hours in this place, lifting the tools from their hooks, imagining them in his father's calloused hands, hoping to feel some small part of his father as the cold tool warmed in his hands.

The interior smelled of pine and fertilizer. He crossed the room to the slab of wood that served as a worktable and slapped his hand on the cool, hard surface. His skin stung, and the silence of the empty room rang in his ears. Matthew oiled the belt on the chain saw and added new plastic string to the weed whacker. He stacked old paint cans and added compressed air to the four-wheeler's tires. All these things he could fix, and it only made him even more aware of the things he couldn't.

Restlessly, Mathew walked out of the shed and headed into the grove of trees separating the house and the barn. The trees were Early Macs but had been called the grandfather trees for as long as he could remember. They seemed to hunch sympathetically over him as he walked among them.

God, do I hire an investigator and try to find her? Should I do what Celie suggested and simply wait? If my mom goes into a depression over this, how do I help her?

He stopped near the base of one of the trees and laid his hand on the scabby bark and closed his eyes. Listening as hard as he could, Matthew waited for some sort of answer. He tried to empty his mind of his own thoughts, his desires, his fears, anything that kept him from understanding God's will. He closed his eyes and concentrated on breathing the cool air. It was harder than usual. He kept hearing the rustle of leaves as a breeze moved through them, the chirping of crickets, and then the soft thud of approaching footsteps.

He opened his eyes. Celie and Toaster were moving toward him. "What are you doing out here?" He was no longer angry. Just tired.

"June fell asleep in the recliner. Toaster and I came looking for you to see if you wanted any dinner." She gave him a small smile. "Toaster tracked you down just like I asked him."

Great. Sold out by his own dog.

In the moonlight, her hair was as dark as the night and her skin was pale and smooth. He set his jaw at the flicker of attraction that shot through him. She was a fashion designer, and he'd never been comfortable in anything but blue jeans. She was ambitious; he wanted only to provide for the family and ensure the financial stability of the orchards for future generations. She was wrong, wrong, wrong for him. He hated the part of himself that knew this and didn't care.

"I'm not hungry."

She shifted her weight. "I'm sorry about Kiera. I know you're worried—I am, too—but she's stronger than you think. I've seen her handle some pretty tough situations. She's got some street smarts, and her faith is strong."

He was about to argue that jumping ship with a man she'd only known for a short time didn't sound like an act of faith or intelligence. However, the retort never left his mouth as the motion detector lights snapped on at the barn. At the same time, Toaster, growling low in his throat, began tugging at his leash.

Matthew's gaze swept the area. The crickets had stopped chirping, and the sudden stillness in the air made the back of his neck tingle. Toaster let loose a series of urgent barks and lunged at the end of his leash.

The motion detector light winked off, but Toaster continued to fuss, ignoring Celie's efforts to calm him. "Take him back to the house," he ordered. The goats started to bleat up at the barn, sending Toaster into another frenzy of barking.

"What's going on?"

"I've got to check something at the barn. Go back to the house." He couldn't waste any more time arguing. He started to run.

"I'm coming, too!"

"No you're not."

But she was. He heard her running closely behind him, then Toaster got under his feet and almost tripped him. They zigzagged among the trees, dodging branches and running half blind through the dark grove. All the goats were bleating like crazy now.

The motion sensors illuminated the area as they stepped within range. He saw the open side door, and his stomach dropped to his shoes. He must not have shut it all the way after he'd fed the animals. He charged into the barn and grabbed the first thing his hands found—a metal shovel off the wall. Gripping it tightly, he crossed the aisle to the oversized stall that housed the goats.

Flinging back the stall door, he took in the cowering goats at the back of the stall and the dark shape of something much larger than a fox. He raised the shovel shoulder high and stepped toward the crouching dark shape. Yelling "Get out!" at the top of his lungs, he swung at the creature's head. It moved like a shadow, though, crossed the stall in a single stride, jumped out the open half of the Dutch door, and disappeared into the night.

For a half second, he saw a coyote, then it disappeared into the night. Its movements scattered the goats who charged out of the open stall door behind him and clattered into the center aisle. Celie screamed. Toaster barked. The goats bleated. Matthew raced out of the stall. "Celie?" He fumbled for the light switch.

Celie stood on top of the old blue tack trunk, holding on to Toaster. The goats had jumped onto the top of two bags of shavings Matthew had stacked. Both girl and goats wore similar expressions of fear.

"Oh Matthew, look," Celie said sadly.

Pressed together as they were, he hadn't noticed until now the blood dripping down the side of the bedding bags. Speaking gently to the animals, he walked over to them. Behind Joy, the female goat, and Lucky, the baby, he saw Happy, bleeding from a gash in his shoulder. Matthew's stomach tightened. Even with just a glance, he knew this wound needed stitches.

He called Doc Bradley's number and left a message with the service. While they waited, he herded the goats back into their stall and fed them additional hay and grain. Happy wouldn't touch a bite, and when Matthew stared into the goat's amber eyes, he saw pain and confusion. His spirits sank even lower when the service called back and informed him that Doc Bradley had been called out to treat a horse with colic.

"What are we going to do now?" Celie asked after he gave her the news.

Matthew shook his head. "I've got a suture kit. The problem is I don't have a tranquilizer or an anesthetic. I could probably stitch him up myself if I could figure out how to hold him still."

"I could hold him."

He almost smiled. "That goat is a lot stronger than you."

Her chin lifted a notch. "Then you hold him and let me stitch him up."

He blinked. "You'd do that?"

She met his gaze. "I don't think we have much of a choice."

"You won't pass out on me, will you?"

She held her hand out. It shook a little, but she said, "No way. I'm a New York City girl. I've seen a lot worse."

He doubted that. She was as white as a sheet. But he didn't see any other way. Retrieving the suture kit, he threaded the curved needle. "You sew the flaps of the skin together, side to side, just like two pieces of fabric. Only you do one stitch at a time and tie off each stitch with a double square knot. Got it?"

She swallowed. "Yeah."

"Okay."

He gathered the necessary supplies and isolated Happy from the other goats. Happy let himself be cornered without too much protest. Matthew grabbed him by both horns and sank to his knees for better balance. He used his body mass to pin the small animal against the barn wall. Celie crept forward with a bucket of water and the sewing supplies.

The goat began to squirm the moment she came near the wound. Matthew spoke reassuringly to the animal and held him pinned against the wall. Happy was anything but happy about the situation, and Matthew had to use all his strength to hold him steady. Celie cleaned the wound and cut the hair around the area as short as possible. "Good," he said and then grunted as the goat strained to free himself. Their struggle made him shift his weight and brought him even closer to Celie, bumping into her as the animal fought to free itself.

"Just like a New York City subway," she quipped, but he thought her voice sounded strained. "I'm ready to stitch him up. Are you sure I should do this, Matthew?"

"Yes. And do it fast." Matthew's arms ached with the strain of holding on to the goat.

He glimpsed Celie's face, white and set, frowning slightly in concentration as she worked.

"One down," she commented.

"Good job." He would have said more, but Happy tried to wrestle free. Matthew tightened his hold, and after a few moments the animal gave up. A bead of sweat rolled down his face. He couldn't spare a hand to wipe it.

They counted time in stitches. There were six of them all together. And when she finally tied off the last one, he felt her tremble against him. "Go on," he said gently. "Get out of the stall before I let go of him."

When she was safely out of the stall, he released Happy,

who lunged away from him and tried to hide beneath the hayrack. Matthew stood and wiped his hands on his jeans. From what he could see, Celie had done a very good job. The bleeding had stopped. He'd still have Doc Bradley check out the goat tomorrow, but for now everything looked good.

Celie waited outside the stall for him. Her eyes were huge in her pale face. She had blood on her hands, on her sweater, all over her jeans. There was a piece of hair that had fallen out of her ponytail. She tried unsuccessfully to blow it out of her eyes.

"You did good in there," he said.

"Thanks." She looked at her bloodstained hands as if she didn't know what to do with them. They shook a little. "Who knew sewing skills would come in so handy?"

He handed her clean gauze. "You could have a whole new career—Celie Donovan, goat doctor."

"I don't think so." But she smiled as she wiped her hands.

He looked down at her. "You were pretty amazing, you know."

"I couldn't have done it if you hadn't kept Happy pinned against the wall."

His arms seemed to open of their own accord; then Celie was somehow inside them, and he was holding her tightly. He rested his chin against the top of her hair. If anyone had told him a month ago he'd be holding her like this—that he'd like holding her—he would have laughed. She relaxed against him. He tightened his arms, closed his eyes, and gave thanks.

sixteen

Celie lined up the side seam and set down the metal foot of June's old Singer. She pressed her foot to the pedal, and the old machine's electric motor revved, then the needle began its high-speed dance. She guided the fabric gently through the machine.

It had been a week since she'd stitched up that goat. Happy was doing well—the vet had praised her work—and Matthew had not only added a latch to the barn door but also covered the open half of the Dutch door in the barn with wire mesh.

She finished the seam and pushed the unwelcome thoughts about Matthew from her mind. "What year did you say this machine was, June? It sure sews well."

"Dermott bought it for me as a wedding gift," June replied. She was dismantling a linen dress that Celie planned to modify. "In its time, it was considered a very good machine."

"It still is." Celie clipped a loose thread and held up the dress. "Would you turn the iron on, June?"

"It's already hot," June replied, fanning herself. "Like today. Here we are, barely into June, and it feels more like August." She glanced at the dress Celie held in her arms. "Oh, that looks nice, Celie."

It wasn't exactly like the hand-painted floral gown destroyed in her apartment fire, but it was a close replica. The fabric had the same Chinese-inspired pattern of magnolia blossoms as the original. It also had a deep, plunging neckline, a ribbed bodice, and a romantic, full skirt. However, Celie had embellished Libby Ellman's original design with delicate green ruffles along the bodice, small pearl buttons, and a cloth flower at the base of the opening in the back.

Pressing the seam open, Celie slid the iron along the fabric.

"Hope so. It's the third time I've made this."

"Third?"

"Libby sketched it the first time, and I made the pattern, but then Mi—" She caught herself just in time. "I mean, then it got damaged at the store, so I took it home and remade it, but that version got burned." Celie adjusted the setting on the iron. "And now there's this one. We'll see if three times is a charm."

"Just exactly how did the original get damaged?" June asked.

Celie avoided her gaze. "I really don't want to talk about it."

"You were covering for someone, weren't you? Does that female who fired you know?"

Celie looked up. Matthew was standing there.

"I came back to get more spacers out of the basement," Matthew explained. "I'm putting them in the Jersey Macs." He looked at Celie. "Nice dress."

She busied herself with hanging it on a garment rack, glad for the change of subject. "Thanks. What are spacers?"

"Some are like clothespins. Some are a couple of feet long. You put them in young trees to get them to grow out, not up."

"You ought to show Celie," June suggested. "She needs a break anyway. We've been working all morning."

"It's okay, June. I know Matthew is probably too busy, and I still have a lot of sewing to do."

"It's not that exciting," Matthew warned. "But if you'd like to see, I'll take you. I could bring you back for lunch."

"Go on," June urged.

Moments later they were bouncing over the uneven path between the trees in Matthew's four-wheeler. Strands of Celie's hair blew out of its bun, and she gripped Matthew's waist as they sped through the orchards. When he finally came to a stop, they were in an unfamiliar part of the property. The trees were much smaller, most about the same size as herself. "Short ones," Celie said, getting off the four-wheeler. "Like me."

"They'll grow," Matthew teased. He handed her a bag of wooden clothespins. "Come on."

They walked over to the first tree. Matthew showed her how to push back the branches growing from the trunk and insert the spacer. "Oh, it's sort of like bobby pins. Only instead of pushing back hair, we're pushing back leaves."

"Branches, Celie," Matthew corrected. "We're training the limbs, not leaves."

"You think it hurts the tree?"

He laughed. "I haven't heard any of them complain." He handed her another spacer and watched as she carefully inserted it between branch and trunk. "So what were you and Mom talking about in there, about you covering for someone else's mistake?"

Celie moved to the other side of the tree. "It was nothing, Matthew."

"It's not nothing if you got fired for someone else's mistake."

The leaves felt slightly waxy between her fingers. She imagined sewing a dress made out of them, lining row after row of them and then stitching them in an overlapping pattern. "I was the one who took that dress home—nobody forced me to do it."

"And why exactly did you take the dress home?"

"Oh Matthew, what does it matter? Done is done."

"I could talk to that woman." Matthew moved a branch that was blocking his view of her. "And explain how you were covering for someone else." He peered through the foliage at her, his eyes a vivid blue, contrasting with the green branches.

She thought of Milah, struggling to make ends meet in her loft apartment in the Bronx and her cute little girl. "That's nice of you to offer but no thanks."

He picked up another spacer and slipped it into the tree. "Why would you want to go back there if they fired you unfairly?"

"They're only one of the top design houses in the world," Celie informed him. "You can't open a copy of *Elle* or *Harper's*

Bazaar without seeing our dresses. And Libby—she drives you crazy—but she's got a great eye."

"I get that George Marcus is a big deal in the fashion world, but why not go out on your own? Start your own label?"

"Lots of people are really good designers, but they can't make it because they have no contacts. And no investment capital. People don't want to take chances on someone who doesn't have a proven track record in the industry."

They finished the tree and moved to another. Celie was getting the hang of putting the spacers in the branches now and worked more quickly. "Did you always know you'd run these orchards?"

"Oh yeah," Matthew said. "My father was very clear on what he wanted. He always felt that God blessed us with this land and said that it's our family's obligation to take care of it."

"But did you ever want to do something else?" She nearly poked herself in the eye trying to look through the foliage at him.

"When I was really little, I wanted to be a baseball player. I was a New York Yankees fan and thought I'd be the next Graig Nettles."

"Who was Graig Nettles?"

"A third baseman. He was an amazing fielder and a great hitter. My dad and I used to watch him play." He pulled a branch down and anchored it with a long spacer. "How about you, Celie? Did you always want to be a designer?"

"Pretty much," Celie admitted. "My mother taught me to sew—she's really talented—and we used to take scraps of fabric and sew gowns for my Barbies. As I got older, we designed dresses for me."

"Oh, so she's a designer, too?"

"Well, she helps my dad run their dry cleaning business. She does all the alterations." Celie frowned. "You know, taking things in and letting them out. Hemming and. . ."

"Your voice changes when you talk about her," Matthew said.

"It does?"

"Yeah. Why are you frowning?"

Celie sighed. She glanced at Matthew's profile. "It's complicated," she said. "My mom is ten times more talented than I'll ever be. She could have been more famous than George Marcus, even." She paused as several low-flying birds passed overhead.

"Being famous doesn't guarantee you'll be any happier than if you aren't."

"I know that." She hesitated. The quiet, serene orchard somehow made it easier to confide in him. "It's just that sometimes I think my mom wonders what her life would have been like if she had put career over family." She had never admitted this aloud to anyone. "Every so often I catch her standing at the kitchen sink, looking out the window with this dreamy expression on her face."

"She made her choice, Celie. I think at some point everyone wonders what their life could have been."

"I know. But she's only told me like a million times, 'Don't settle.'"

"That sounds like good advice."

Celie stepped back from the tree and shielded her eyes with her hand. "I think it means, 'Don't end up like me.'"

He turned slowly. "And what's so bad about her life?"

"She lost her dream," Celie said sadly.

"Are you so sure?" He was looking at her with a strange expression.

"I think so. And it didn't help that I got fired. She was devastated for me." She looked long and hard at him. "Hasn't there ever been anything you really wanted but couldn't have?"

A guarded look formed in his eyes. "Of course," he said. "Lots of things. But it doesn't mean those were the right things for me." He wiped his face. "Nobody likes disappointments, but I believe God allows them into our lives for a reason." He gave her a crooked smile. "I know it's hard, but I believe God wants us to have life in its fullest. Sometimes we can take a wrong turn—make the wrong choice—but He always gives us another chance to get back on the path He means for us to take."

He was right, and it was something to think about. As they walked back to the house, she thought about the turns a life could take—about right ones and wrong ones and sometimes how hard it was to know the difference.

seventeen

Celie parked the Honda in the outdoor lot at the Danbury train station and took the 9:55 a.m. into Manhattan. Even traveling off-peak, the compartments were crowded. She had to take a seat that had her riding backwards, sitting next to a young man with three rings in his eyebrow and across from a woman typing furiously on her laptop.

She clutched her sketchbook and watched the buildings give way to greenery as the train sped down the New Haven line. She could feel the anticipation of being in the city warring with the unexpected longing for the orchard—and if she were honest, for Matthew.

She thought about the dresses, carefully laid out on the rack above her. They weren't exact replicas of the ones lost in the fire—she could have made them exact replicas, but she'd followed her instincts, adding embellishments, lengthening a hemline here, and tailoring the sleeves there. She was proud of them. There was a good chance Libby Ellman and George Marcus would see and be willing to forgive her. And if this wasn't enough, she had the drawing of the green dress in her sketchbook.

When they reached Grand Central, people still moved in a slow, hot shuffle through the tunnel and into the station. Uno and Sudgi waved at her from the coffee shop, and Duncan McCloud, wearing the familiar NYPD uniform, still stood at the exact spot next to the 42nd Street exit.

Her Jimmy Choo boots—a little more battle-scarred than the last time she'd been in the city—clicked smartly as she slipped into the steady stream of people heading east on 42nd Street. She breathed in the stale, slightly smoky scent of city air and smiled at the sound of a car's horn, protesting the bumper-to-bumper traffic. All around her, buildings and skyscrapers towered, filling every bit of available real estate.

On the corner of 42nd and Fifth, she spotted James standing beside the halal cart. His light gray pinstripe suit was new, but the ubiquitous cup of coffee in his hand wasn't.

"James!"

He grinned when he spotted her. "You're a sight for sore eyes," he said, hugging her. "Let me help with those." He took the garment bags out of her hand.

She was wearing a slim pencil skirt made from some of the material she'd purchased at Fabric Attic and had paired it with a tangerine blouse she'd pulled out of the church box and remodeled. "You're not so bad yourself," she said. "Calvin Klein?"

"You like it?"

"Love it. You're sure having lunch with me won't get you into trouble?"

"Are you kidding?" James joked. "They can't tell me who I can and can't be friends with." He reached for her arm with his free hand. "Come on, I'm starving."

They bought plates of spicy dark chicken meat covered with an even spicier green sauce and walked the remaining blocks to the New York Public Library. Celie's heart swelled at the sight of the massive stone lions flanking the steps to the building's entrance. They found an empty table in the courtyard. Celie shooed away the pigeons and took a seat.

As they ate chunks of the savory chicken, James quickly brought Celie up to speed at George Marcus Designs. "Got a lot of orders from the spring show at the Javits, but now Libby is freaking out because George hates everything she's shown him for Paris. Everybody's working late and on weekends and grumbling because she keeps changing her mind about everything."

"Sorry to hear that." Celie gestured toward the garment bags. "Maybe those dresses will help."

"I hope so." James washed down his chicken with a long

drink of coffee. "You're really missed."

Celie pulled out her sketchbook. "Missed so much that she might be interested in seeing this?" She slid the opened book over to James, who moved his lunch to make room.

"It's gorgeous." He angled the page into the light. His gaze lingered on the page. "Maybe the best thing you've ever done."

"Gorgeous enough to get me my job back?"

James's mouth twisted. "Celie, designing wasn't what got you fired. You broke company policy by taking a gown home without permission. You don't know how close you came to George pressing charges against you. Fortunately, Milah stayed up for two days straight and came up with a couple of substitutes."

Celie tossed a piece of pita bread to a begging pigeon. She wanted to tell James exactly why she'd taken the hand-painted gown home in the first place, but she didn't see what good it would do, other than make her feel better. "I'm sorry about what happened, James. You have to trust me—it wasn't completely my fault. All I want is my old job back. Will you please help me?"

"Sweetie, I'd swim the Hudson River in December for you. Of course I'll help. But it will take time." He ripped the page out of Celie's sketchbook then stared at the exposed page. It was a pencil drawing of Matthew with the apple orchards in the background.

"Who's this guy?" James lifted his gaze from the page to study Celie's face.

She felt herself blush. "That's Matthew."

"That's Matthew?" James laughed. "The guy who doesn't like you? I thought you two were cat and dog."

"Oil and water, actually." Celie tugged the sketchbook out of her friend's hands. "But now we're friends. I think." She heard the defensive note in her voice. "It's complicated."

"Sure," James agreed. "Love is complicated."

"I don't love him."

"That's not what this drawing says. It's not what I see in his eyes."

"I don't see anything special in this drawing. And Matthew most definitely doesn't love me."

"If you believe that," James scoffed and pushed his glasses more firmly onto the bridge of his nose, "I've got a very nice bridge to sell you."

&

It was nearly eight o'clock when Celie parked her Honda in the Patricks' driveway. The wind had picked up. She heard it in the heavy rustle of leaves in the trees. A flowerpot had fallen, and she bent to straighten it as she stepped onto the porch steps. Toaster barked a welcome at the sound of her footsteps on the porch.

Matthew opened the front door before she even knocked. The sight of him holding on to the squirming dog made her heart thump in her chest. All at once it felt as if it'd been ages since she'd seen him, and it felt so good that if she hadn't had two shopping bags in her hands, she might have done something crazy—like hugged him.

"Hi," Celie said, looking up into his rugged, sun-tanned face.

"Welcome back." Matthew pulled the door wider. "Mom's in the living room," he said, although this information was redundant. The volume of the television could be heard clearly. What was less clear was whether Matthew seemed glad to see her. His mouth had that tight *Celie, why did you move that candlestick?* look to it. His blue eyes, however, seemed to say, *I'm glad you're safely back.*

From her recliner, June punched the MUTE button on the remote control and grinned up at Celie. "Did it go all right? I want to hear everything."

Celie set the shopping bags down and plopped onto the adjacent club chair. Toaster immediately launched himself into her lap and jumped up to lick her face.

"Toastie!" June ordered. "Leave the girl alone. Get down. Why aren't you minding me, Toastie?"

"It's okay, June."

June called the dog again. This time Toaster obeyed. With an audible grunt, he heaved himself into her lap. "My goodness, this dog has put on weight," June said. "How did you get to be such a plumpie, Toastie?"

"Because you give him too many cheeseburgers," Matthew observed dryly.

"You think so?" June asked very innocently.

"I don't think so. I *know* so."

Celie laughed. A bigger gust of wind rattled the windows before heaving itself silent. She automatically glanced at the darkness outside, grateful for the safety of the old house, the coziness of the living room, and the sounds of Matthew's and June's voices.

"Animals shouldn't be too thin," June argued. "People, either. Did you get anything to eat for supper, Celie?"

"I grabbed a sandwich at Grand Central," Celie assured her. She bent over to retrieve the shopping bags. "I brought you both back a little something." She handed June the first bag.

"You didn't have to do that," June admonished but reached eagerly into the bag. "Oh," she exclaimed, pulling a pair of silver chandelier earrings from their tissue wrapping. "They're beautiful. Thank you, Celie."

"I thought the blue stones would match your eyes," Celie said. She handed Matthew another bag.

His dark eyebrows drew together in a puzzled look that quickly turned to pleased surprise as he pulled out a new coffee mug with a big red apple on it. "The Big Apple—New York City," he read. His gaze shifted to her. "Thank you, Celie."

Their gazes met, and her heart started to thump. "It's to replace the one I broke. Glad you like it."

He set the mug on the table but continued to trace his fingers along the smooth rim. "I'll use it tomorrow morning."

Celie thought about his lips touching that cup and felt her heartbeat kick up another notch. Lucky mug. That she could be jealous of a coffee cup was ridiculous. She wasn't a country girl. She liked short skirts, high heels, makeup, and pedicures when she could afford them.

"Now tell us about the meeting," June prompted. "You and James."

"Well," Celie began, "James liked the sketch. He said he'd show it to Libby when the time was right."

June clapped her hands. "It'll all work out. I just know it! Did you invite James and the big muckety-mucks to the Castoffs to Couture show?"

"Yes."

Another gust of wind hit the house, and the lights flickered and then died. Startled, Celie gripped the armrest of her chair, straining to see beyond the wall of darkness around her. The blackness was absolute, and the sudden silence told her the power had gone out. A few seconds later, though, the lights came back on.

"We'd better get the lanterns and some candles, Matthew, in case we lose power again." June already had gotten to her feet and was leaning on the cane. "I guess the weatherman was right for once. We're in for a doozy of a storm."

eighteen

Celie woke in the darkness to the sound of rain. Not a steady little beat on the roof but a full-fledged assault that pounded down on the house as if it intended to pulverize it. She pulled the warm comforter higher under her chin and listened to the wind slash sheets of water against the windows.

The clock said five thirty as she turned on the china lamp and swung her legs out of bed. Her bare feet registered the drop in temperature as she slipped on a pair of jeans and a gray NYU sweatshirt leftover from Kiera's college days. She tied her hair back and headed down the stairs.

Matthew helped June down the stairs shortly after Celie had started breakfast. "Sounds like a monsoon out there," June said, raising her voice to be heard above the drumming on the roof.

"I'm just glad it's not hail," Matthew said, pouring himself a cup of coffee. He was holding the new mug, and Celie was disproportionately pleased to see it in his hands.

June frowned. "I was going to get my hair done today." She patted her hair, pulled back in its usual, neat bun. "I am so tired of this hairstyle. I want something more contemporary. Something more youthful."

"You should reschedule, Mom." Matthew added two heaping spoonfuls of sugar to the dark brew. "We'll be lucky to keep our power."

"I don't want to reschedule," June snapped. "It took me two weeks to get this appointment with Clint. Jeremy is coming over this afternoon, and I look like the wreck of the Hesperus."

Matthew shook his head. "You look fine. It's a good day to stay inside. The McGillis pond is sure to flood. I don't want either you or Celie on the road today."

101

"You could take me," June argued. "The pickup has good water clearance."

"I'm going to be working on the tractor's engine," Matthew said. "And I doubt very much that Jeremy will come out in this weather anyway."

Celie watched the edges of the scrambled eggs start to solidify.

More rain slashed against the windowpanes. She understood June's desire to make herself attractive. Yesterday Celie had walked past her favorite place to get her nails done, and it had taken extreme effort on her part not to go inside. "Maybe I could take you, June, in Matthew's truck."

Matthew swallowed his coffee the wrong way. Coughing, he waved away June, who reached over to thump him on the back. "It's a stick shift," he managed at last. "I could just see the two of you ending up in the middle of the McGillis pond, sinking fast."

Celie set a platter of eggs on the kitchen table. She'd never driven a manual transmission vehicle, but Matthew shouldn't just make assumptions like that about her. "How do you know I can't drive a stick?"

The corners of his mouth lifted a fraction. "Because you're a city girl."

She waved the serving spoon at him. "Exactly. Driving in New York City is not for the fainthearted. For your information, I can be a very aggressive driver."

Matthew's lips stopped curving. "That does not make me feel better and has nothing to do with the ability to change gears."

"All I need is one gear," Celie argued.

"Let's just do it," June urged. "I can talk you through it."

"Neither of you is going anywhere," Matthew said loudly. "Do I have to take the keys, or do I have your word that you won't go anywhere?"

"Oh take the keys, then," June said irritably.

The minute Matthew left through the back door, June

turned to Celie. "He's being totally unreasonable, isn't he? It's not even raining that hard."

It was pouring rain and still so dark outside that she couldn't see the orchards. Celie sensed pointing this out to June wouldn't help. "Well, it's a good day for sewing. We've got a lot of work to do."

June followed her reluctantly into the dining room. She sat on one of the mahogany chairs and stared out the window. Celie saw the unhappy pucker to her lips and remembered the pink floral fabric she'd bought a few weeks ago at the Fabric Attic. Retrieving it from her room, she went to work.

June sewed seams on the old Singer and from the sound of the engine had the pedal plastered to the ground. They worked for almost an hour, then June rose restlessly to stand at the window, peering out into the gray morning.

"Light's on in the shed," June commented. "Matthew'll probably hole himself in there for hours." She glanced at her watch. "Still time to make my appointment."

"Hmmm." Celie snapped off a bit of thread. She held up June's new skirt. It still needed a zipper and hemming, but she liked the shape and the way the fabric hung. She'd wanted something romantic, something soft and feminine for June. "What do you think, June? You like it?"

June turned at the sound of her voice, and there was a determined glint in her eyes. "I love it, Celie, and I know just what would go perfectly with it."

"A pink blouse?" Celie suggested. "Something with a V-neck?" Something fitted would work best. For being so tall, June really was tiny. Maybe a narrow belt around the waist.

June smiled. "Not a shirt or a sweater. A new haircut." The glimmer in her eyes grew stronger. "I think there's a pair of spare keys to the truck in the junk drawer in the kitchen."

❧

Matthew wiped his hands on a rag. He had a carburetor problem. Even after removing the parts, cleaning them thoroughly, and replacing them, the engine continued to race, even in the lowest gear. He probably needed at least one new cylinder.

Overhead, the rain continued in a steady beat, a pleasant drumming noise. It no longer sounded as if a waterfall were pounding the roof of the building. The storm was passing, just as predicted. There'd probably be some flooding and slight wind damage to the trees, but overall they'd been fortunate. Thank God.

Matthew remembered the storms of his childhood. His mother humming a cheerful tune as she set out the candles, filled the bathtubs with water, and turned on the battery-powered radio.

He and Kiera had made tents in the living room and counted the seconds between the flashes of lightning and the crack of thunder. They'd seen some bad storms, too. Hail stones as big as a man's fist, a hurricane that had thrown a tree through the bay window, and several times June had sent them to the basement when the sky turned green and the clouds created suspicious-looking formations.

There were no funnel clouds, though, as Matthew hiked the distance from the shed to the house. He hung his dripping slicker on a peg and greeted Toaster who danced around him, wagging his tail.

The mudroom held a vague chemical odor. Frowning, he looked around for the source of the smell. Nothing seemed out of place. The washer and dryer were empty, the double sink was scrubbed clean, and the usual containers of detergents and cleansers sat with their caps securely tightened in their places. Ammonia, he decided. The ladies had been cleaning.

He stepped into the kitchen. The chemical smell disappeared, but to his disappointment, nothing delicious bubbled on the cooktop. But this didn't surprise him entirely. It was barely three o'clock in the afternoon.

"Matthew? We're in here!"

Matthew followed his mother's voice into the living room

and stopped beneath the arched entrance. Company. He hadn't known they were expecting anybody. Hadn't seen any cars. A tall, ash-blond stood with her back to him. The unfamiliar woman wore a floral skirt that floated just below her knees and a pink sweater that was the same shade of flowers in the skirt. "Hello," he said politely.

The ash-blond woman turned, and Matthew's jaw dropped.

"Matthew," his mother said, striking a pose and positively beaming at him. "What do you think?"

Think? His mind went blank. He couldn't seem to wrap his brain around the image of June standing there looking nothing like herself. He'd grown used to the sight of her dressed in comfortable sweat suits, her silver hair pulled back into a tight bun. He couldn't remember the last time he'd seen her wearing a skirt. It shocked him further to realize that, even at seventy, his mother had nice legs.

If this wasn't enough for his brain to process, there was the hair. It looked different, slightly on the blond side of silver. She'd cut it, too—short layers framed her face. And she had light, wispy bangs.

"Do you like it?" June prompted, turning slowly.

Matthew crossed his arms, frowning, as it occurred to him that June had kept her hair appointment after all. After he'd specifically told her to stay home. She knew how dangerous the road became when it flooded. What had she been thinking? "I told you not to go out today."

"I didn't," she said smugly.

"Then how did you get new clothing and a new hairdo?"

Grinning from ear to ear, she pointed to Celie. "Celie did this. We had so much fun, Matthew. I had some old hair dye in my bathroom, and the rest is history. Do you like it? Every time I walk by a mirror, I surprise myself."

She surprised him, too. It made sense to him now. The chemical smell in the mudroom had been the hair color. They'd had to use the downstairs sink because June still had trouble doing stairs.

His mom touched her cheek. "She even did my makeup. I haven't worn foundation in years."

She didn't need to be wearing it now, either. Matthew pinned his gaze on Celie. His blood started to boil. He remembered the weekend Kiera had come for a visit wearing a dress that was much too short and tight. She'd had on heels so high that it'd almost put her on eye level with him. "My friend Celie designed this just for me," she'd said, spinning slowly.

"Isn't she beautiful?" Celie asked, turning to him, smiling proudly.

"She was beautiful before, too," Matthew said sharply. He forced a calm note into his voice. "Can I see you in my office, Celie?"

"If you're going to offer to pay her," his mother admonished him, "I've already offered, and she's refused. I told her all this would have cost me at least a hundred dollars at Clint's."

"I'm not offering her money." Matthew marched off to his office. He closed the door behind them and only then allowed some of the fury to release itself. "How could you do that to my mother?"

Celie's cheeks paled and then turned red. "She looks great. Why are you so upset?"

Matthew paced the small, wood-paneled office that had been his father's and his father's before him. "Couldn't you see that she was beautiful before?" He came to a stop a few feet in front of her. "Why do you always have to change everything around you? People. Furniture. Clothing. Even the dog has to have a designer coat."

She planted her hands firmly on her hips. "What was I supposed to do, Matthew? She was going for the spare set of keys to the truck. You know your mother. This was the only way I could think to stop her."

"She was bluffing." Matthew's voice rose, but he couldn't seem to help it. "With her bad hip, she can't hold down the clutch. She couldn't have gone anywhere unless you drove her."

"Oh." Celie seemed momentarily taken aback. "She was going to cut and color it anyway. It's not a capital offense to change a hairstyle, Matthew. That hair dye wasn't so old."

He glared at her. He had about a foot and more than a hundred pounds on her, and yet she met his gaze unflinchingly. "I liked how she looked before better."

"Get over it." Celie's eyes flashed. "June likes it, and I do, too." Her chin lifted a notch. "Maybe what bothers you the most is you're afraid that Jeremy is going to like it as well."

"I don't care if Jeremy likes it or not." His mother and Jeremy? Not a chance. They were old friends, and Celie had no right suggesting otherwise.

"Why do you think your mother was so set on getting her hair cut today?"

"You should mind your own business." He struggled to hold back his temper and thought he might have a brain hemorrhage with the effort required.

"What's wrong with helping your mother feel more attractive?"

He took a deep breath. "You start changing the way people look, you change their lives, and maybe their lives don't need changing."

"Maybe you should let them be the judge of that."

"Maybe you should stick to sewing dresses."

The rain drummed steadily down, filling the silence in the room. The mahogany-paneled office had always seemed small, a tight fit for the built-in bookcases and the keyhole desk. It felt huge now, cavernous, and Celie seemed a mile away from him, although he could have reached out and touched her if he wanted.

Matthew pushed his hands through his hair. All he was doing was trying to protect his family. Kiera had been hurt, and he wasn't about to stand still and let the same thing happen to his mother.

"All I'm saying is no more makeovers. Not my mother, the dog, the house, the horse, or the goats." Had he left anything out? It was hard to think straight with all these emotions buzzing around his head like a swarm of angry bees.

"Fine," Celie practically spat the word. Her eyes were almost black, and her small fists were clenched.

He watched her walk away from him, her shoulders stiff and her spine as straight as if he'd jabbed her in the back with a poker. She took the steps at a slow jog and disappeared down the hallway. He heard the click of a shutting door. He turned to find June staring at him. Her lips twisted in concern. "What was that all about, Matthew?"

He looked at the silver chandelier earrings hanging from her lobes. She'd always worn the pearl studs his father had given her as a wedding gift. Pushing his hands in his pockets, he shook his head. "Nothing. Nothing important."

nineteen

Jeremy arrived the next day shortly after ten o'clock. "There's still a few inches of standing water on the road," he explained as Celie greeted him at the door. "Don't know why the town doesn't do something about the way the McGillis pond fl—" The word died on his lips as June stepped into the hallway.

"June," Jeremy began, working visibly to push that one word through his lips. "June," he repeated, his gaze locked on June's tall, thin body. "You are stunning. Simply stunning."

"You look pretty nice yourself," June said. "I like the green suspenders."

"And I like your skirt."

Celie put her hand over her mouth to keep from laughing. Thank heaven Matthew wasn't here to see the two of them gazing at each other like moonstruck teenagers.

"Celie made it for me. You really like it?" Her cheeks turned the same pink as her sweater.

Of course he liked it. Celie could hardly keep herself from prompting Jeremy, who couldn't seem to tear his gaze from June. "I love it," he said.

Celie beamed. Jeremy was reacting just the way a man should act when an attractive woman dressed up for him. Awestruck. Slightly bemused and highly appreciative.

"Shall we get started then?" June led the way to the dining room. "Celie and I made good progress yesterday. We finished off two cocktail dresses." She gestured toward two dresses—both former bridesmaid dresses—hanging at the front of a crowded garment rack.

Jeremy slung his jacket over the back of a chair and rolled his sleeves to his elbows. Celie noticed that he took a seat across from June instead of stationing himself at the ironing

109

board as he usually did, and he couldn't seem to stop looking at June.

"The ladies on the luncheon committee are meeting today to decide the menu," Jeremy said. "We can fit about a hundred people in the church basement."

"A hundred people!" Celie had pictured maybe fifty. "You really think that many people will come?" Jeremy pushed his hands through his thick white hair, looking more than ever like a combination of Einstein and the sweetest grandfather in the world. "I think double would come to the rummage sale, and who knows how many people would buy tickets to the luncheon if we had more space."

"We ought to move it outdoors," June stated. She was cutting out the lining from a man's brown suit. "We could fit more people under a tent."

Jeremy shook his head. "I thought about that, but the road construction on South Main won't be finished by then. It'll be too hard to hear the announcer over a jackhammer. Plus, if we use the parking lot, what will people do with their cars?"

"We should have it here," June declared. "In our front yard. People could park in the field across the street, and we could have the show under the grandfather trees."

Jeremy sat up a little straighter. His bushy white eyebrows rose almost to his hairline. "You know, that might just work. We haven't started advertising yet, the clothing already is here. . ."

"And the orchards would be a perfect setting," Celie finished. She could already imagine the branches in the apple trees heavy with bright red apples, their trunks wrapped in white tulle. She saw ladies sitting among the trees at round tables with crisp white linen cloths and vases stuffed with wildflowers.

And then she imagined Matthew's face, scowling down at her. *Why'd you have to change them*, he'd say. *Weren't the trees pretty enough for you to begin with?*

"The trees would be full of apples," June agreed, her hands

pausing with the scissors still buried in the fabric. "The Early Macs would be ready to harvest. We could probably sell some. That'd raise some more money for the church."

"I like this idea," Jeremy said. "Having the fashion show in the orchards has a lot more atmosphere than the church's basement. Don't you think so, Celie?"

Celie drew the thread through the needle. "Are you kidding me? It would be great. But someone besides me ought to ask Matthew."

June read Jeremy's puzzled expression. "The two of them were in Matthew's office, fighting like cats and dogs, and then neither of them would eat a bite of dinner." Her gaze turned to Celie. "What did he say to you last night?"

So Matthew had been upset enough about their argument not to eat. The knowledge made Celie feel unaccountably satisfied. "We just disagreed about things, that's all." She knotted the thread, unwilling to risk hurting June's feelings by sharing Matthew's true opinion of the older woman's makeover.

"What things?" June pushed a pair of reading glasses higher on her face. "What things, exactly."

Celie shrugged and began to tack down the lapel of the jacket in her hands. "You know. The way I always change things. Same old. Same old."

"Oh." June sighed. "She's talking about the furniture we rearranged. I should have told you to return the quilt to the back of the sofa." She shook her head. "You'd think he'd be ready to put aside those memories."

What memories? Celie's hands tightened on the jacket. She all but held her breath waiting for the older woman to continue. The only sound June made, however, was the whisper of her scissors cutting through cloth. Celie cleared her throat. "Umm, what memories?"

June put the fabric aside. "Old, old ones. Bittersweet ones."

Celie didn't want to pry, but she wanted very much to know. She pulled the needle in and out of the brown fabric, glancing up when she felt June's gaze on her.

"When Dermott started having digestive problems," June began quietly, "he went to the doctor and was diagnosed with colon cancer. Of course by then, the cancer had already spread. The doctors knew it was hopeless, but they wanted to give Dermott as much time as they could, so they did a couple rounds of chemotherapy and radiation. Took a terrible toll on him." Her gaze went to Jeremy. "You saw what it did, the weight he lost."

Jeremy nodded. His gray eyes looked sadder than Celie had ever seen them. "Dermott kept fighting, though," he said. "He went through it all with honor."

"Never complained," June agreed. "Never lost his faith. If anything, it made his relationship with the Lord even stronger. He got thinner and thinner until he was just a shadow of himself. Always cold. At night I'd light a fire and he and Matthew would wrap up in that old quilt and sit on the couch together. The two of them." She paused and smiled fondly. "Snug like two bugs in a rug."

June looked at Celie but seemed to be seeing Matthew and Dermott snuggled up together as they had been all those years ago. "Dermott would read Matthew stories from the Bible, and then they'd talk about them. About what they really meant. Dermott could explain things as well as any preacher I've ever heard." She smiled. "Matthew soaked it all up like a little sponge. Dermott held on as long as he could, but eventually the Lord took him home.

"Afterward, most nights Matthew would wrap himself and Kiera up in that quilt and read the Bible to her. She was just a toddler when he started, and they did it for years—I don't know when he stopped—but ever since then, we've kept that quilt folded on the back of the sofa."

"June, that is the most beautiful story I've ever heard." Celie had to dig her fingernails into the palm of her hand to keep from crying. "I'm so sorry I moved that quilt."

June shook her head and smiled. "Don't be sorry. This

house needed a change. I just didn't realize how much we needed it. I guess you get used to living a certain way."

"I'm putting that quilt back immediately." Before June could protest, Celie leaped to her feet and hurried up the stairs to retrieve the quilt from her bedroom. She kept thinking of Matthew and Dermott together, then Matthew and Kiera, and this one quilt that had bound them together.

As she carefully folded the quilt and draped it exactly the way she'd found it over the edge of the sofa, she thought of her own parents. The traditions she'd grown up with—the week in July at Madison Lake State Park, Christmas caroling, the crazy birthday hat—the one with the singing fish—that each of them wore at his or her birthday dinner. She longed suddenly to talk to her parents, especially her mother, and resolved to call them later.

She lifted down the mirror from the mantelpiece and put back the portrait of Great-Grandmother Caroline. The candlesticks went back to the dining room. In their place she carefully put the knickknacks and hurricane lamps in their original positions.

"You don't have to do that, honey," June called out. "Come back and sit down with us."

Celie shook her head. "Not until I finish. I can't remember—where was the china shepherdess before we put her on the bookshelf?"

"In Kiera's room."

Celie hurried upstairs. When she returned, June and Jeremy had their heads bent toward each other in an easy, conversational way. "Jeremy was telling me some very good news!" June exclaimed. "Tell her."

The old ladder-back chair groaned as Jeremy shifted to see Celie more easily. "Emily would like to be in the Castoffs to Couture show."

"I wrote her measurements down for you," June added, waving a piece of paper at Celie. Celie looked at the numbers on the paper and felt a wave of envy. It didn't help that June and Jeremy were raving about how beautiful Emily was, too—all tall and blond. She fought the urge to crumple the paper. What was wrong with her? She'd never been envious of Kiera's measurements—or good looks. So what was the difference? *You're jealous*, a voice in her head said. *Emily is Matthew's former girlfriend.*

She put the piece of paper on the table. "I'd love for Emily to be in the show. I'll find her something really great to wear."

"Oh, she'll be happy with anything," Jeremy said. "She's not hard to please. Did I mention she's coming home for the Fourth of July and also taking all her vacation this summer here?"

"That's wonderful," June cried. "Sounds like she misses this old town. You think she might be ready to come home for good?"

"It's what I've been praying for," Jeremy replied.

"I'll start praying for this, too."

Celie was spared from making any comment as the doorbell rang. She jumped to her feet, glad of the excuse not to hear any more about Emily Taylor.

"Shirley Elliot's here already?" June shook her head. "The time just flies by."

&

A small group of women—and Jeremy Taylor—sat sewing in the dining room when Matthew got home. He was in no mood to socialize and headed straight for his office, barely pausing to say hello. After the fight he'd had with Celie last night, he had no desire to face her anytime soon.

To his surprise, his office door was shut and someone had taped a sign to it. MODEL'S CHANGING ROOM.

Matthew gritted his teeth. He knocked loudly, intending to tell whoever it was to find a new place to change. The words died on his lips when the door opened and Lilac Westover, the minister's wife, stood there in a black tuxedo with a frilly white shirt sticking out of the jacket.

He blinked, his feet rooted to the ground more securely than any of the grandfather apple trees in the orchard. In thirty-something years, he'd never seen Lilac Westover in anything but an ankle-length skirt and blazer. The sight of her in a tux made him want to rub his eyes. Not because she looked funny—just the opposite. She looked great. It made him realize how talented Celie actually was to turn something that had probably been a man's tux into something so feminine.

His mother tapped him on the shoulder. "Matthew. I need to talk to you." She glanced around him at Lilac. "Oh! You look amazing! Everyone, look."

Lilac moved gracefully into the foyer, and everyone peeked around the boxes and hanging clothing in the dining room to see her. The ladies in the dining room twittered approval. He recognized Jill Lane, the town's one and only policewoman, and Susan Grojack, retired now but with those hawklike eyes that missed nothing. She'd been his seventh-grade science teacher and had called on him to read the most embarrassing slides during their human reproduction unit.

Esther Polino, the town's librarian, moved past him, something slinky and purple in her petite arms. She tossed him a grin before disappearing into his office.

"I want to ask you something," his mother said, "and I want you to think about it before you answer."

In other words, she was about to ask him to do something he didn't want to do. He frowned. His gaze moved of its own will to Celie, willing her to look at him then looked away when she did.

"Matthew?" Her cane thumped on the wood floor. "Are you even listening?"

He forced his gaze back to his mother. He was getting used to the feathery bangs on her forehead, the slight wave in her hair. He couldn't deny she looked more purposeful. Happier, too, than she'd been in a long time. The harsh words he'd exchanged with Celie echoed uncomfortably in his head.

"With more space," she continued, "we could expand the show and bring in more revenue for the church. You wouldn't have to do much. We'd have the caterer bring in the tables and Shirley Elliot's pretty sure her husband can have his sound team wire some loudspeakers in the trees."

They wanted to move the show to the orchards. Matthew's gaze traveled to the racks of clothes. He wasn't much of a fashion expert, but even he could tell these remakes of other people's castoffs were good. Really good. He'd encouraged this project in the first place and was more than willing to help make it a success. Besides, he felt badly about the things he'd said to Celie. "Okay," he said.

"Okay?" his mother echoed in disbelief. "You really mean that?"

The women in the dining room stopped chatting. Even the sewing machine went still. "You can have the show in the orchards," Matthew confirmed. "Just as long as it doesn't interfere with the picking schedule."

"It won't. We'll have it early. August instead of September," June assured him, a triumphant smile stretching across her face. "You hear that, everyone? Matthew said yes!"

A loud cheer went up. Matthew shrugged off the thanks. He fervently wanted to get out of the house before Esther Polino stepped out of his office in the purple number. He didn't want to see the librarian in anything but her customary turtlenecks and slacks.

He retreated through the house, pausing in the living room. Something looked different. The mirror was gone, and the knickknacks on the mantelpiece were back. The furniture also had been returned to its old arrangement. And the blue quilt with the Log Cabin pattern hung neatly over the back of the couch as if it had never been moved.

The room looked almost exactly the way it'd been before Celie arrived. Matthew glanced at the curtains, drawn to protect the antique furniture from bleaching. Everything sat in its right place, but nothing felt right to him anymore. The room seemed almost gloomy to him. He wondered if it'd always been like this and he was just seeing it now.

Isn't this what you wanted? For her to stop changing things? He rubbed his face hard. It was exactly what he'd wanted, and yet having it brought him no pleasure. No pleasure at all.

twenty

Matthew hadn't said anything about the changes to the living room, but Celie thought he approved. The next morning, he handed her a cup of tea with extra sugar in it, just the way she liked it. "You up for a surprise?" he asked.

"If it's a good surprise." Celie smiled. Now that she knew the story behind the quilt, she was as anxious as he seemed to be to put their argument behind them.

"It's a good one," Matthew assured her. "Give me about an hour and meet me on the front porch."

Celie didn't know what to expect, but it certainly wasn't the sight of him driving Bonnie hitched to a shiny black buggy down the long driveway. She shielded her face from the morning sunlight. He was smiling at her. Hmmm. He didn't do that often enough.

"Want to go for a ride?"

She was already halfway down the porch steps.

It seemed as if she'd stepped back a hundred years in time as she climbed into the shiny black buggy and settled on the smooth leather seat. "Central Park and Fifth," she quipped.

"Would you settle for a really nice ride through the orchards?"

"Are you kidding? I'd settle for down the driveway." Celie could hardly keep herself still on the seat. "I've always wanted to do this."

June waved them off from the porch. "You all be careful," she shouted. "Been a long time since Bonnie's pulled anything but grass out of the ground."

"You want to come, June?" Celie called back. "I'll squish over. There's room."

"No thanks." June pulled a weed from one of the hanging

pots overflowing with bright red geraniums. "I'm going to bake some double chocolate brownies. Have fun, though."

Matthew slapped the reins lightly over Bonnie's broad haunches, and the buggy rolled forward. Celie squealed, earning her an amused glance from Matthew, who couldn't possibly know of all the times she'd sat on a bench in Central Park and watched the horse-drawn carriages roll past. She'd planned to splurge on a ride when her parents came to visit.

They crossed Route 303, passed through a long, swinging gate, and followed the bumpy dirt road into a forest of pear-shaped trees. Apple trees. Celie was beginning to recognize the oval shapes of the leaves, although she still couldn't tell a Jersey Mac from an Empress.

It'd rained the night before, and the tree limbs still hung heavy with their darkened, water-soaked leaves. Bonnie plodded along, occasionally trying to steal bites from the trees. "What kind of apple trees are these?" She didn't really care, but she didn't want to ride in silence, either. What she really wanted to say was that she admired the way he'd held the family together after his father's death.

"Early Macs," Matthew gestured to the right. "The Paula Reds are a couple of rows over."

End of conversation. She was seated right next to him and yet felt like there was a big elephant on the bench between them. The elephant was their fight. She supposed she should just put what'd happened behind her. Pretend it'd never happened.

Celie sighed. "About your mother's makeover," she began. At the exact same time, Matthew said, "About yesterday."

They looked at each other and laughed. Celie took a deep breath. "I'm sorry about changing things in the house, and I promise not to cut your mother's hair again."

"I overreacted. Mom's hair doesn't look that bad."

"What?" She'd heard him clearly but couldn't believe he meant it.

The color darkened beneath his tan. "I may have gotten a

bit carried away the other day. You didn't have to rearrange the furniture again. I was just getting used to it."

She'd seen his anger, his protectiveness, his family loyalty, even his sense of humor—but an apologetic Matthew? This was new. She liked it.

Bonnie continued walking down the path. The reins looped loosely over the mare's back. Matthew didn't seem to notice how the horse kept ripping leaves from the trees. He seemed more interested in looking at her. Being pressed against the hard wall of his side gave her an opportunity to study his perfectly formed lips, the straight line of his nose, the thick fringe of his black eyelashes.

Celie's heart began to beat harder. It was her turn to try to explain things. "I should have understood what I was doing before I moved things around." She pushed her bangs behind her ear. They immediately fell to her chin. "When I was about fifteen, Grandma Rosie came to live with us. She had lymphoma and needed some help. She was this great lady, Matthew, always trying to give you something every time you saw her—food, a book she liked, something sparkly she saw when she was out shopping." Celie's throat grew a bit tighter. "When she couldn't get out of bed, I used to cut her hair and sew her pretty nightgowns and bathrobes. It made her so happy, Matthew, to look pretty. She told me I had a gift for design—and with that gift came a responsibility. 'We're blessed, Celie,' she told me, 'so we can be a blessing to others.'"

Bonnie's walk slowed then stopped all together. Matthew didn't seem to notice. He was staring at her, and suddenly he was leaning toward her. And she was leaning toward him. Her heart beat even faster. *What are you doing?* a voice all but shouted in her head. *You're going to let yourself fall for a guy who lives on an apple farm in the middle of nowhere?*

It would be crazy to kiss him. She'd die if she didn't.

The buggy suddenly lurched forward, throwing them both off balance. She started to laugh and then gasped as a cold shower rained down on her. It was over as soon as it started. She looked up. There was an enormous branch above her head, and beads of water still dripped from the leaves.

She looked at Matthew. His skin gleamed from the unexpected bath, and the shoulders of his blue T-shirt clung to his body. He was grinning from ear to ear. Before either of them could say anything, the buggy lurched forward another foot. There was a tearing noise in the leaves, and then another shower of cold water rained down on their heads. Celie screamed at the shock of it hitting her skin.

If that wasn't enough, she had suddenly become eye level with a thick tree branch. Clearly Bonnie had taken advantage of their preoccupation and pulled them off the trail. Each time she took a bite, it shook the leaves and released the rainwater from the night before.

Bonnie grabbed another branch. It was a big one. Celie screamed. "Get the reins, Matthew!" A fresh shower pelted down on them. "Come on, Matthew!" He was laughing too hard to do anything about it. She looked at him, water turning his chestnut-colored hair a deep brown and his mouth wide open, showing very white, very even teeth.

She could fall for this guy, Celie realized. Fall deep and hard if she let herself. Her heart told her he was a good man as well as an attractive man. But could she really picture a city girl like herself living on the orchard forever?

twenty-one

His mom was sitting in the porch swing sewing when Matthew dropped Celie back at the house.

"How did you all get so wet?" his mother asked, gazing at them somewhat suspiciously.

Celie looked at Matthew, and they both laughed at the same time. Matthew felt himself turn red. "Bonnie took us on a side trip under some of the trees."

"Oh," his mother said. "Is that so?"

"Yes," Matthew said, not trusting himself to look at Celie.

"Well, Matthew, maybe she wouldn't want to eat so many leaves if you fed her more."

"I guess you're right, Mom." Matthew played along. "Maybe you should come to the barn and supervise."

"I guess I should," she replied.

Matthew blinked in surprise. He'd only been joking. Yet his mom was walking down the steps and right over to the buggy. "I'll drive," she said.

Matthew had to half lift her into the leather seat, but once inside she picked up the reins. He'd barely made it back into the buggy before she slapped them across Bonnie's back. "Giddyap," she said.

He gave one last look at Celie as she disappeared into the house, then he turned his attention back to his mother, who was urging Bonnie into a trot. "Move along," she urged the heavyset horse.

"What's the rush?" Matthew wanted to say but stopped, not wanting to spoil his mother's fun.

When they reached the barn, he helped her out of the buggy. For a long moment, June gazed at the goats in the pasture. "They look good," she commented. Her hands were clenched into fists, and the lines in her face cut deeply into skin that seemed even more fragile in the morning light. "I thought I'd see more of a scar on Happy's back."

"Celie did a great job sewing him up." He saw the emotion in his mother's eyes and wanted to reassure her. "Come see the latch on the door and the wire mesh I put on the windows."

He quickly unhitched the horse and led her into her stall. His mother watched from the middle of the aisle, her eyes semiclosed. She was taking long, slow breaths with obvious pleasure. "Don't breathe like that near the goats' stall," he joked, "or you'll faint."

"I like how a barn smells," she stated.

Matthew watched her gaze go to the steps of the hayloft. He felt the familiar tinge of guilt. Two long hours. Two long painful and helpless hours, wondering if help would come. He stepped closer to her. "Anytime you want to smell the barn, I'll bring you up. We can take the four-wheeler."

"Thank you, Matthew. But I'll walk."

Matthew blinked in surprise. "What? I mean, that's great." He turned the question over in his mind before he asked it. "But why now?"

She stared at him with a glint of determination in her eyes. For a moment Matthew glimpsed the mother of his youth standing there, running the orchards with a sure hand, dealing with everything from hurricanes to helping him and Kiera with homework.

"Six months ago," his mother said slowly, "I broke my hip. I thought the best of my life was over. All I could see in the future was how I would become more and more of a burden to you and Kiera. I didn't see that the Lord was preparing me for something else entirely."

"What do you think He was preparing you for?"

His mother smiled. "The next phase of my life."

Matthew shifted uncomfortably. What exactly did that mean? "What are you talking about, Mom?"

She shook her head a little cryptically. "Things are

happening here, Matthew. Good things. God things. I wasn't ready to receive those gifts before, but I think I'm ready now. It's amazing how He can take a worn-out life and make it feel like something new."

She wouldn't say more, and after a short time, he walked her back to the house. She wanted to sit on the porch swing by herself, and he went inside to get her a cup of tea. The house was quiet when he came through the mudroom door. Celie had her back to him with the black telephone receiver pressed tightly to her ear.

"I know you don't want to hear this, Kiera," Celie said, "but I think you're rushing into things. This guy may be the perfect one for you, but you've only known him a couple of weeks."

Kiera? A surge of blood rushed to Matthew's face. He clenched his fists as relief collided with worry, joy with anger.

"Kiera, how do you know this isn't a rebound thing?" Celie paused. "Jumping ship with the cruise's photographer sounds romantic, but basically, what do you know about this guy?"

Matthew knew he should make his feet move, his voice work, do something instead of just stand there.

"What about your life here?" Celie demanded. "You have a family who's worried about you. I'm worried about you. When are you coming back?" Another pause. "Please don't hang up. I'm not lecturing you. I'm trying to help you."

Matthew couldn't wait any longer. He stepped forward, but before he could reach Celie, she said, "You're what? Kiera! Please talk to your mother or to Matthew. I'll get them. It'll take a second. No! Don't hang up." A brief pause. Celie's voice changed, pleading now. "Give me a number then where we can call you."

He knew Kiera's response by the sudden slump in Celie's shoulders. She stood, staring at the receiver and shaking her head. He cleared his throat loudly.

She whirled around, her eyes wide and startled. "How long have you been standing there?" And before he could even reply, she said, "That was Kiera. She, ah, couldn't stay on the phone long, but she wanted me to tell you and June that she's fine."

Matthew nodded.

Celie's oval face creased unhappily. "Actually, she's better than fine." She paused again and studied his face. "Maybe you'd better sit down, Matthew."

"Just tell me," he ordered gruffly.

"Well, she's in love." Celie winced as if saying the words gave her physical pain. "And she's engaged."

❧

June set the kettle on the burner and turned the gas on full blast. "Please tell me again what Kiera said."

Celie repeated the conversation for the third time. Matthew paced across the kitchen. Every so often he'd stop, start to say something, then shake his head. Celie had never seen his jaw clenched so tightly.

"We're starting a prayer chain," June announced. "I don't see any other thing we can do."

"I'll help make calls," Celie offered, jumping at the chance for action.

"Just what are we praying for, Mom? To be invited to the wedding?"

"Stop being silly, Matthew." The kettle whistled a piercing note. "We're praying for God's will." June poured the boiling water into the mugs. "For all we know, this man might be the right one for Kiera."

Matthew snorted.

"You sound exactly like Happy," June pointed out, stirring sugar into her tea. The humor fell flat, and June's hand trembled slightly as she set the spoon in the sink. "Are you sure Kiera knows about the fashion show, Celie?"

"Positive."

We're having a big fashion show at the orchard. I have the perfect dress for you.

Sorry, Celie, but Benji and I need to get to know each other as a couple before we let anyone else influence our relationship. We need more alone time together.

June sipped her tea. "I would have thought she'd come back for the fashion show, if nothing else. She's loved modeling since she was two years old."

"Unfortunately she's still acting like she's two years old," Matthew snapped. "Who goes on a cruise ship to Mexico and ends up engaged to the ship's photographer?"

Celie winced at the disapproval in his voice. "Maybe June's right. Maybe this guy is the right one for her."

"A ship-jumping, unemployed photographer?" Matthew snorted. "He's probably some kind of fortune hunter who preys on vulnerable women."

"I admit he sounds like a leech, but we don't know for sure." June met Celie's gaze. "We should start by calling Lilac Westover. She'll start the chain."

"I'm going out." Matthew crossed the room in three powerful strides. The door to the mudroom opened and slammed shut. Celie would have put her arm around June, but something in the older woman's eyes stopped her. She reached for the telephone instead.

twenty-two

Kiera might think she was in love, but when it came to men, she didn't exactly have the best track record. In her bedroom, Celie pinned a waistband to the bodice of her couture dress. It was well past eleven o'clock. A gentle breeze lifted the sheer curtain, cooling the room.

She loved Kiera like a sister. At the same time, Celie wanted to stick a pin into her. Jolt some sense into her.

How many times had Kiera thought she'd been in love? At least four times. All attractive, older, charismatic men who told Kiera they loved her and then dumped her a week later. As far as Celie could tell, the only man who'd ever treated Kiera decently was Aaron Buckman—the hardware guy—and by the third date, Kiera was calling him boring and not returning his calls.

Celie pushed another pin into the fabric, taking care not to let the charmeuse slide. The weaving had come out even better than she'd imagined. Usually the feel of the silk soothed her—allowed her to dream about catwalks and fashion shows, the look on Libby Ellman's face when she offered Celie back her job. Tonight, though, the silk felt too rich, too opulent. She would have traded it in a heartbeat for a plane ticket to bring Kiera home.

She glanced at the clock, nearly midnight, almost time for her link in the prayer chain. She knelt on the braided rug by the side of the bed and closed her eyes.

Thump.

Her eyes flew open. The noise had come from downstairs, and it sounded like something, or someone, had fallen. Her heart began to pound. June had enough mobility to get herself up and down the stairs. What if she'd gone downstairs to get a snack and fallen?

She raced down the semidark hallway and down the stairs. At the foot she paused, struggling to see in the pitch-black. A small sliver of moonlight barely gave her enough light to make out the dark shapes of the furniture.

She couldn't remember where the light switch was and started toward the thin silhouette of a standing lamp when she heard a soft rustling noise coming from the kitchen. She spun around and groped her way to the back of the house. Beneath the arched entrance, she paused. A dark figure sat hunched over on the hardwood floor.

Illuminated by the stove light, Matthew crouched on the floor mopping up a dark liquid puddle in front of him. "Matthew?"

He jumped at the sound of her voice. "You startled me."

"Well, you *scared* me," Celie echoed. "I thought June fell."

Her gaze searched out his features, blurred in the dim light. His eyes, stripped of their color, were nonetheless beautiful. She felt an odd stirring in her stomach and a pleasant tingle in her veins.

"I couldn't sleep," Matthew admitted. "I thought a glass of warm milk would help, but then I tripped over Toaster's bone." His gaze swept over her, taking in her jeans and T-shirt. "What are you doing up so late?"

Celie shrugged. "It was my turn to pray for Kiera, but then something went *thump*."

"I kicked Toaster's bone by accident into the cabinets."

"Why didn't you turn on the light?"

"I thought I could see just fine."

"Let me look."

He held his foot up, showing off a very large big toe. It was a manly toe, fat but with a neatly trimmed nail. Right now it was held in such a way as to suggest it was a very painful manly toe.

"I'll get some ice." She retrieved a pack from the freezer, set it on his foot, and joined him on the floor. "Leave it on for twenty minutes."

"You don't have to hang out here," Matthew said in a low rumbly voice. "I don't think it's broken or anything."

Celie settled herself with her back to the pine cabinets. "If I don't stay here, you won't ice it."

He didn't contradict her. "Besides," Celie added, "it's cooler downstairs, and I can just as easily pray here." She paused. "You could join me if you want."

He did. Even after the ice pack had been long removed, he seemed content to sit on the wide planks of the floor. The heat coming off his body contrasted to the summer breeze blowing in through the open window, bringing with it the sweet scent of the orchards and the tinkle of porch chimes.

Somewhere in the night, an owl hooted and she jumped. "City girl," he said, but she heard the smile in his voice.

She didn't protest when he slipped his arm around her or move an inch when she saw the dark shadow of his face moving toward her. Her arms seemed to lift of their own accord and find their place behind his neck. In the moment before his lips touched hers, she felt an incredible sense of rightness, of completeness. She closed her eyes.

And he kissed her.

twenty-three

Celie melted into his kiss. She felt his hands gently cupping her face and the warmth of his body pressed closely to her own. Everything tumbled around her. She couldn't think. Couldn't move. Couldn't do anything except hold on to Matthew.

His hair felt like silk threads in her hands. And then a voice in her head practically shouted, *Are you crazy? Do you want to end up like your mother—looking out windows and wondering what could have been?*

It took all her strength, but she managed to pull away from him.

Matthew gazed down at her. "Hey," he said, his voice full of wonder.

Her heart began to thump at the sound of that one word. Her gaze went back to his lips, but that incessant voice inside her head pointed out that Matthew lived on an apple orchard and she wasn't exactly a farmer kind of girl. She liked stores and shopping, the bustle of a city and having lots of people and action. "I'm sorry," she whispered. "I can't do this."

Matthew smiled gently. "You were doing just fine. Better than fine."

She slid a few inches away from him. "Please, Matthew. I can't." She wouldn't let herself look at him. "This never should have happened. I. . .I'm sorry." Before he said anything else or, heaven forbid, kissed her again, she got to her feet and ran out of the room. He didn't come after her.

The next morning he made bacon and eggs and teased Celie about sleeping late, although it was barely six thirty. It was like nothing had happened. Celie was relieved. She also was unaccountably disappointed.

The next two weeks passed in a blur of marathon sewing sessions, meetings with ladies from the church, and trips to the Fabric Attic for more supplies. Celie spent the mornings and afternoons altering clothing for the Castoffs to Couture show and the evenings working on her silk dress. The days grew longer, and the temperature settled in the high eighties.

The Fourth of July arrived, and Matthew took Celie and June to see the town fair and fireworks show. They all squeezed into the front seat of his truck. He drove them to the town park, the lush, green ball fields now filled with vendors selling everything from hot dogs to jewelry. Happy shouts overflowed from several huge inflatables for the kids, and a man dressed up as Uncle Sam walked around on stilts.

They walked to a temporary wooden stage first. June had brought a chocolate cream pie for the pie-eating contest and wanted to drop it off before they wandered around the fair.

Seated behind a table and writing on a clipboard, Celie recognized Susan Grojack. The tall, silver-haired woman had come to June's house several times to help with sewing and also was one of the models.

As June and Susan visited, Celie's gaze wandered around the area. The fair already had been going on for hours, and a good-sized crowd filled the park. She saw a little brown-haired boy with his family. Her heart gave a tug at the sight of the wand of cotton candy that was almost as big as the little boy.

And then her heart skipped a beat as she spotted a familiar blond head bobbing in the crowd. Kiera? Celie strained for a glimpse of the woman's face then sighed in disappointment.

It wasn't Kiera. This woman had her build and coloring, but her features were different—stronger. Plus, Kiera would never have worn Keds or gone out without makeup. The blond, however, headed straight for them, picking up speed as she went.

"Matthew!" The woman cried and launched herself into his arms.

"Emily Taylor," June cried in delight. "As I live and breathe. Come give this old woman a hug."

Either Emily was hard of hearing or just plain chose to ignore June's request. The statuesque blond remained wrapped around Matthew as if she were drowning and Matthew were her life preserver. Truth be told, Matthew didn't seem to mind. From what she could see of his face, he was smiling.

"I'm so glad to see you." Emily finally emerged from Matthew's arms, gave June a much gentler hug, and looked back at Matthew as if she'd like to jump right back into his arms. So this was Emily Taylor. The girl who had broken Matthew's heart. No wonder. What man could resist those big blue eyes and dimples?

"You, too, Em. You just get in?"

"Yes, late last night." Her voice lowered, and her gaze moved to include June. "Look, I know about Kiera. I've got an investigative reporter at the *Hartford Courant* making some phone calls." She turned to June. "Try not to worry too much. We'll find her."

"Bless you." June patted the tall blond's cheek. "Sure is good to see you, honey."

"You too, Mrs. Patrick. You look wonderful. I like your haircut."

"Celie did it." June's fingers closed around Celie's arm, gently squeezing. "Oh. You haven't met yet, have you? Emily Taylor, this is Celie Donovan—a friend of Kiera's."

"Oh I know all about you," Emily cried, turning the full wattage of her dazzling white smile on Celie. "My dad told me all about the fashion show you're putting together!"

Celie winced at the strength of Emily's grip. "Nice to meet you."

Emily brushed a long strand of hair behind her ear. "Isn't this fair great?"

Celie glanced down at Emily's blunt-tipped fingers. Not a scrap of polish on them and no rings, either. She shifted on the wedged heel of her espadrilles and pondered the unpleasant possibility of Emily joining them for the day.

"Girls!" Susan Grojack's strident voice interrupted Celie's thoughts. "Girls! Could you please come over here? I need your help."

Celie hurried over to the registration table, eager to escape Emily.

"The pie-eating contest is supposed to start in ten minutes, but we don't have enough entries for the women's category," Mrs. Grojack said, holding up her clipboard as if it were evidence. "In order for this to count toward the state pie-eating competition, we need seven entries, and I've only got five. Would you girls be willing to help me out?"

Celie exchanged glances with Emily, who shrugged good-naturedly. "What kind of pie is it?" Emily asked. And then, before Mrs. Grojack could answer, said, "Oh, who cares? I'll do it."

Celie glanced up at the long narrow table on the raised platform. When she, June, and Matthew had arrived, it'd been empty, except for a checkered tablecloth. Now five women sat side by side, wearing bibs and very serious expressions.

"I'll do it, too." She didn't actually have to be competitive. She could just sit there and nibble whatever they put in front of her.

She signed the necessary forms and listened to Mrs. Grojack explain the rules. The winner would be the one to eat the entire pie the fastest. Celie thought about the mountain of whipped cream she and June had put on their chocolate cream pie. She didn't even want to think about the calories.

She took a seat at the very end of the table, and Emily sat next to her. Celie tied a tacky paper bib with lobsters on it around her neck. She weighed the fork in her hands and stared at the audience. Matthew and June waved from the front row. June scrunched up her face and gave Celie a nod. *Be tough*, the look seemed to say.

Next to her, Emily nudged her. "Use your hands instead of

the fork. And look out for Grace Higgins. She was fifth in state last year. I don't think she chews the crust."

Celie laughed. "I'm not going to try to beat anyone." As the pies came out, people in the audience began talking. "Grace Higgins has it made in the shade," a man in a checkered red shirt said.

"Grace Higgins," another voice echoed. "In forty-three seconds flat."

Celie looked down the table at Grace Higgins. She was a heavyset woman with small eyes and thick, frizzy hair. Right now she was flexing her arms, stretching as if she were getting ready for a wrestling match.

"Emily Taylor can take her," Matthew yelled. "Go, Em!"

Go, Em? Celie felt a stab of disappointment. Not *Go, Celie?*

"Emily Taylor," another male voice shouted. "Three minutes, forty-two seconds."

"Who's the cute little gal sitting next to Emily?"

Celie sat up a bit straighter. Little gal? She was five foot four—in heels, that was.

"That's the city girl—the one who's staying with the Patricks," someone explained.

"Oh, a city girl," a voice said.

Celie bristled. Just because she was a city girl, it didn't mean she couldn't hold her own in a pie-eating contest.

"You might want to move your seat a little to the side." Emily tested the space between herself and Celie with her elbow. "This could get kind of messy."

Celie moved her chair a little farther from Emily, who was now grinning in anticipation of the event. The referee asked if all the contestants were ready. Emily said, "Ready for you to buy me dinner, Matthew Patrick—if I win this!"

Celie's eyes narrowed. She glanced sideways at Emily. The blond was bigger, but Celie thought she could take her—if she wanted to. And that's when she realized she very much wanted to.

The referee's whistle blew, and Celie dug into the pie.

twenty-four

"Anyone ready for a break? I just pulled some double fudge brownies out of the oven." June stood in the doorway of the dining room, holding a plate.

"Brownies?" Claire Innetti laughed. "Not chocolate silk pie?"

Celie groaned. It'd been two weeks, and everyone was still joking about her second-place finish in the pie-eating contest. "Please stand still, Mrs. Innetti," she requested, "so I don't catch your skin when I zip you up."

She braced herself and tried to erase the gap between the sides of the zipper. Mrs. Innetti was trying on a yellow cotton sundress with an empire waistline. June had been correct—Celie should have added a good inch to the measurements she'd been given. A fresh bead of sweat popped out on her forehead, despite the fan going full blast.

"Everybody in town is still talking about it." Mrs. Innetti, who was the senior pharmacist at CVS, met Celie's gaze in the antique standing mirror. "Word is, you're going to state next year."

"No way." Celie tugged the fabric hard, and the zipper slid up the dress. "What I'm going to do is never eat chocolate silk pie again. Now what do you think of the dress?"

She stared at Mrs. Innetti's reflection. The halter neckline drew attention away from the tall brunette's broad shoulders, and the seaming beneath her bust showed off her curves without making her look heavy.

"I think," Mrs. Innetti said, "you could've taken a couple seconds off your time if you hadn't used the fork."

"Celie definitely was the neatest eater." A note of pride entered June's voice.

Celie had a dim memory of shoveling huge mouthfuls of

pie into her mouth and an even dimmer memory of chewing. She mostly remembered the startled sideways glance Emily Taylor had given her, though, when she'd realized Celie meant business.

"Most competitive match people have seen in years," Mrs. Innetti continued. "A real horse race. You and Emily Taylor neck and neck, right up to the end."

Celie smiled a little. She might not have beaten Grace Higgins, but she'd edged out Emily Taylor by 4.3 seconds. She wouldn't soon forget the look of surprise on Matthew's face.

"The dress," Celie said, firmly steering the conversation back where it belonged. "You want me to let it out a little?"

Mrs. Innetti turned sideways to see another angle. "Oh definitely not. It fits perfectly." She sighed in pleasure. "I never would have thought I could wear something like this and not look like a ripe summer squash."

"You definitely don't look like a ripe squash," Celie assured her. "Now how about shoes? A strappy sandal. The higher the heel, the better."

"I don't know." Mrs. Innetti frowned. "Haven't worn them in years. . .but I guess I could try." Her chin came up a notch. "And Celie, after the show, I'd like to buy this dress."

Celie smiled. "Great."

"I'll put you down for it." June named an amount and laughed as Mrs. Innetti eagerly nodded. "Celie, we're going to be sold out before the show even begins."

❧

A few weeks passed. The end of July came. Matthew brought home fresh corn from the farmer's market in town. He roasted it on the grill, and they ate ear after ear with sweet-cream butter. June provided a steady supply of pies, cookies, and cakes, which she gave to all the women from the church who showed up day after day helping sew and press, put together sample outfits, and organize the clothing which would be sold in the rummage part of the church event.

One afternoon after she'd just finished a fitting, Celie slipped upstairs to her room. She pinned her hair off the back of her neck and waved her hand to try to cool off a little. She had a little free time before the next model came for a fitting, so she took the green couture dress out of the closet.

She'd finished it two nights ago. Examining it on the hanger, she *knew* it was the best dress she had ever designed. The green and yellow strips of silk wove together in just the right places to enhance a woman's bustline, and the skirt was neither too full nor too clingy. It fell organically, creating a graceful silhouette. She moved the hanger and watched the fabric float. She couldn't look at it without thinking of the orchards.

Returning the dress to the closet, she decided to give James a call. He picked up on the second ring. "I've been meaning to call you," he said.

"Did you get the tickets to the fashion show? You're coming, right?" She wanted to ask if Libby or George had seen the design for the green silk but couldn't quite bring herself to ask.

"Wild horses, kid, couldn't keep me away."

Something was wrong. She could hear it in his voice. "What is it, James?"

There was a long pause. Celie felt her heart sink.

"I don't know how to tell you this, but yesterday morning I saw Milah making a dress almost exactly like the one in the sketch you gave me."

The realization sank in slowly, but when it did, Celie crumpled to the floor. "Libby stole my design?"

"She denied it, of course," James said sadly. "She's changed enough details to make it seem like a different dress, but it's your design." He paused. "I'm so sorry, Celie."

Celie hung up her cell phone and wished she'd never made the call in the first place. A curious numbness settled over her. Libby had stolen the design. Worst of all, there wasn't anything she could do about it. She wanted to scream or stomp her feet or break something. Anything but stand here and know that she'd been a fool. She ran down the stairs and out the back door. The ground passed in a green blur as she sped across the lawn and into the grove of apple trees. She wanted to outrun the knowledge of what Libby had done, outrun the pain of betrayal and the loss of a dream. She wanted to run until the world changed into a better place, and she didn't hurt anymore.

Why had God let this happen? Was she so far off the path He wanted her to choose that it had come to this?

Only when her lungs ached and her legs felt as heavy as concrete did she allow herself to slow to a jog, and then even this became harder than she could maintain. She slowed to a walk then came to a complete halt.

Celie sank to her knees in the grass. She put her face in her hands. *What do I do now, Lord?*

She heard the dull sound of feet thumping on the path, and then Matthew said, "Celie? What's the matter?"

Leaping to her feet, Celie brushed the grass from her shorts and wiped her cheeks. She tried to tell him she was fine, but her facial muscles weren't working right. Her smile kept crumpling.

"Talk to me. Whatever it is, we'll fix it." His blue eyes fixed on hers as if he were trying to pull the answer out of them.

"I called James." She heard her voice shake. She didn't want to tell him, but she couldn't not tell him, either. "My couture dress. Libby stole the design."

His brow furrowed. "What do you mean she stole the design?"

"She copied it but then changed enough details so she could call it an original."

"Can't you sue her? You have the original hanging in your closet!"

Celie shook her head. "It'd be my word against theirs. And right now I don't have any clout."

"Wouldn't James stand up for you?"

"If he did, he'd lose his job. What would he do then?"

Matthew seemed to consider this for a moment. "He'd find another job. It's a matter of honor, Celie. He shouldn't let them do this to you."

"I was stupid, Matthew. I shouldn't have let James show that design to Libby and George." She blinked back tears that continued to fall anyway. "I was sure they'd want not just the dress but me."

Matthew patted her back awkwardly, as if he wasn't sure how to comfort her. "We can't let them get away with this, Celie. We've got to fight them."

"How? I can't pay for a lawyer. And even if I could, I wouldn't win. This sort of thing happens all the time in the fashion industry." She wiped her eyes with her sleeve. "I'm just an idiot. Why am I so stupid, Matthew?"

"You're not stupid. You have a trusting heart. There's a big difference between those two."

Celie laughed bitterly. "It doesn't matter. I'm finished."

"You're not done." Matthew raked his hand through his hair. "We'll figure something out."

"Like what?"

He handed her a crumpled but clean handkerchief. "You could stay here."

Celie wiped her face. "And do what?"

He shrugged. "Start your own Internet business, get a job in town, or Mom had this idea a couple years ago to start a mail-order apple butter business. We've still got the canning jars in the garage. You could help her."

He actually thought she should consider a career in apple butter? "All this time," Celie sputtered, "you've known me, and you don't see who I am? You don't understand what sewing means to me? You think I could can apples for a living?"

Matthew held up his arms in mock surrender. "I'm just giving you suggestions. You don't have to take them."

She kicked a clump of grass. "What if you couldn't grow apples? What if someone took away your orchards and told you to work in a factory?"

He frowned down at her. "But would it be so bad to stay here? Is working in Manhattan really what you want?"

Celie didn't pause to listen to the small voice in her heart that said maybe it wasn't. Maybe what she wanted was standing right in front of her. She thought only of her mother, standing at the kitchen window, looking out at lost dreams. "Yes," she replied firmly. "It's exactly what I want."

twenty-five

If Manhattan was what Celie wanted, Manhattan was what she was getting. Matthew, however, had no idea how to give it to her. He just knew he had to find a way. When he returned to the house, he found his mother standing at the railing, tapping her cane in impatience. Her face creased in worry.

"What's going on? I saw Celie take off like a cat with its tail on fire."

She leaned on her cane, a sure sign she'd been on her feet too long. Matthew led her to the swing. "The designer in New York City stole her dress design. She's not getting her old job back."

His mom stamped the porch floor with her cane. "I knew those people couldn't be trusted." She sighed. "The poor girl. No wonder she took off like that. You didn't just leave her alone in the orchards, did you, Matthew?"

She gave him a reproachful look. So did Toaster.

"She wanted to be alone."

His mother shook her head. "When something upsetting like this happens, people say things they don't mean. Women, especially, say they want to be alone, but they actually mean the exact opposite."

Matthew stifled a groan. June was only trying to help, but right now he didn't need a lecture on understanding women. "She's fine." He kept his tone neutral to hide a pain he wasn't quite letting himself feel. Celie had been very clear on what she wanted. It wasn't this orchard. And it wasn't him. "If she isn't back in an hour, I'll go get her."

His mom nodded. The slight pucker to her mouth relaxed, and she patted the seat next to her. "I wonder what she'll do."

141

When he didn't comment, she said, "Stop pacing, Matthew. You're making me and Toastie dizzy."

He hadn't even realized he'd been walking back and forth. When he stopped, it felt wrong. His hands and feet seemed to hang uncomfortably from his limbs. He gazed as far into the orchards as he could see for a flash of Celie's yellow shirt.

"Maybe this is a blessing in disguise." June patted the empty space on the porch swing. "Maybe God has something even better in store for her. Come sit, Matthew."

"I'm fine."

"You're like a cat on a hot tin roof."

"Please stop the cat analogies. I'm going to take the four-wheeler out." He'd check the south field, which was as far from the grandfather orchards as he could get. The wind blasting in his face would clear his head; it always did.

"Just tell her how you feel," his mother stated firmly. "Don't be like me."

He stopped cold. He understood neither statement. A ray of sunlight striped the porch step. It felt like a line he wasn't quite ready to cross. "Just what do you know about how I feel about Celie?"

"Quite a bit."

Matthew turned slowly. She was rocking the swing gently, a soft smile on her face. "I feel it," she said. "When you're around her, you come alive. I've never seen any two people as much aware of the other in my life."

"You're wrong."

"Don't be like me, Matthew. Don't deny what your heart knows."

Matthew frowned. The urge to escape faded as he studied the harsh planes of his mother's face and the proud, determined set of her shoulders. "What are you talking about?"

"Jeremy Taylor." Her chin lifted. "We've waited a long time—and I've prayed a lot about this—and we're going to dinner next week." As if this wasn't crystal clear enough, she added, "We're going on a date, Matthew." She held her hand up as he started to speak. "You probably think I'm too old. You probably think I'm dishonoring your father."

Matthew let his breath out slowly. "I don't think that. And you don't need my permission to date him, if that's what you want."

"I'm not asking for it," his mother said gently. "I just don't want to hurt you, Matthew. You've looked after me and your sister and this farm better than anyone could have asked."

"You're not hurting me."

She rose from the swing awkwardly and came to stand beside him. "No one can ever take Dermott's place, but I have feelings for Jeremy, too."

He shifted his weight. What did his mother want from him? His blessing? A tug of loyalty to his father warred with his genuine desire to see his mother happy. He sighed. "He's a good man, Mom. Just don't expect me to call him Dad." He smiled to let her know he was only joking.

"I think I always knew he was there for me, waiting." His mother's eyes half closed in remembrance. "I'd see him sometimes in church looking at me. . . ."

"I'm okay with you dating him. We don't have to go into detail."

Her eyes snapped open. "I was going to explain that I turned away, Matthew, because I knew what the look on Jeremy's face meant." She kept her gaze on his face. "Sometimes we know what's right for us. It's right under our noses, but it scares us, so we don't do anything about it."

Matthew didn't want to see any truth in her words. "Thanks for your concern, Mom, but let's just leave the romance stuff to you and Jeremy."

"Don't wait too long to tell Celie how you _feel_," she warned. "You'll lose her if you don't say anything."

Matthew gave an indifferent snort, but his gaze strayed back to the orchards. He thought about her out there, making decisions he couldn't control, wanting things he couldn't give her.

In the distance, trees swayed gently in the summer breeze. The vastness of the land, its beauty—even the great aloneness of it—stirred through him. He understood why this life might be right for some people and totally wrong for others. Like Kiera.

He'd known Kiera dreamed of far-off places, but selfishly he'd wanted her to stay tied to the family through the land. After his sister had moved to New York City, he'd encouraged her to visit then tried to make the time they all spent together a positive experience. The simple truth, however, was that he couldn't hold the family together any longer. He'd lost Kiera, was losing Celie, and even June seemed ready to embrace a new life.

What am I supposed to do, God?

&

When his alarm went off at four thirty in the morning, Matthew sat up, relieved he no longer had to lie in bed trying to sleep. He'd gone over and over his plan, rehearsed every detail. There was nothing left to do.

His only suit—a dark gray color—stood out in a closet filled with work shirts and jeans. It was wool and much too hot for a day sure to reach the midnineties, but he thought it would be better to dress up. He chose a blue and red striped tie and pulled it tight around the collar of his white shirt. He stuffed his feet into a pair of stiff leather shoes, usually worn only to weddings and funerals, and tied the laces taut.

Toaster barked once as he crept down the stairs. He heard his mother hush the dog, then the house went quiet again.

Mom and Celie, he wrote on a scrap of paper, *I'll be gone for the day. Thomas and his crew are mowing around the grandfathers today, so they'll be nearby if you need anything. Don't wait dinner for me, Matthew.*

The moon shone a beacon of light as Matthew stepped quietly out of the house. The soles of the leather shoes felt slippery on the surface of the gravel driveway. The orchards were lost in the night, but he paused to peer into the darkness. *Heavenly Father, please bless this day and grant me the words and strength to serve Your purpose.*

He got in the car and did not look back as he drove away.

twenty-six

Several times during the next two weeks, Matthew disappeared for the entire day. June clammed up whenever Celie tried to question her. But once she'd let something slip about train schedules. Celie wondered if he was going to Hartford to see Emily Taylor. She buried herself in sewing and preparations for the rummage sale.

Celie was even more confused when Emily Taylor came back into town. True to her word, the blond reporter had taken off the two weeks prior to the fashion show as vacation. She called Celie the day she arrived and scheduled a fitting for the next morning.

When Emily arrived, Celie had a beaded black cocktail dress waiting for her. Emily grinned from ear to ear when she saw it and lost no time in putting it on. She had just stepped out of the changing room when Matthew walked into the dining room. "Emily? Thought I saw your car."

"Matthew!" Barefoot, Emily practically sprinted across the room to hug him. Although Matthew's face turned bright red, he didn't step away from her.

"Do you like the dress, Matthew?" Emily asked. She turned slowly to give him the full view.

How could he not like what he saw? Celie put her hands on her hips. Emily was drop-dead gorgeous. She watched Matthew wipe his face with his hand. He glanced briefly at Celie then back at his voluptuous former girlfriend. "Yes."

"It needs some alterations." Celie nearly dragged Emily back to the mirror and away from Matthew.

"Doesn't this dress remind you of the one I wore at the Great Gatsby party?" Emily didn't wait for Matthew to answer. "Remember? You wore your grandfather's pin-striped suit, and we won first place for the best costume?"

Matthew chuckled. "Oh yeah. We hid Dillon Mayfield's mattress in the hayloft."

"He itched for a week," Emily said, winking.

Celie gritted her teeth as Emily and Matthew continued their stroll down memory lane. The back of the dress was a little loose, so she reached for the pincushion to mark the alteration needed. Emily was still talking about the costume party as Celie pulled out a pin. The shiny metal seemed to wink in the light. It could look like an accident, a simple slip—one little poke—and Emily would be firmly detoured off memory lane.

"Are you free for dinner tonight, Matthew?" Emily asked. "A couple of things I'd like to talk to you about."

"Sure," Matthew said.

That woman was making a move on Matthew! The hand with the pin seemed to move of its own accord toward Emily. Celie jerked it back right before she poked her. What was she thinking? Her hand was shaking and had almost stabbed Emily Taylor. What did Celie care if the two of them wanted to rekindle their friendship and possibly their romance?

Evidently she cared a lot. But in a way, it helped her come to a decision.

ta

"I'm leaving tomorrow, June." Celie tied a length of white tulle ribbon around the base of the grandfather apple tree. "Right after the show."

"You're what?" June dropped the basket of scissors and ribbons but made no move to pick it up.

Around them, preparations for the next day's fashion show continued in full speed. A group of men standing on ladders hung speakers in the trees. Caterers rolled out large folding tables, and a small group of women stood at the beginning of the runway, talking and laughing.

Celie watched a range of emotions play across June's weathered face—surprise, disappointment, uncertainty, and then finally, understanding. "You sure?"

"Positive." Celie retrieved the scissors and spools of tulle. "I'm sorry just to spring this on you, June, but I didn't know if there would ever be a good time."

"Why?" June's mouth puckered. "Why don't you stay longer?"

"I just can't." Celie found her gaze drawn to Emily Taylor's bright blond head. She was standing with the other models who were waiting their turn to practice walking down the runway. More than ever, Celie suspected Emily was more interested in Matthew than she was being in the fashion show. Even as jealous as she was, Celie couldn't help but think Emily fit Matthew's world a lot better than she ever would. The best gift she could give either of them was to step out of the picture.

"Where are you going to go?"

The worry in June's voice broke Celie's revelry. "Centerville."

"You're going to work at your parents' dry cleaning business?" June clucked her tongue. "I wish you would reconsider. Stay here awhile longer."

"I appreciate the offer, June, but my mind is made up. Besides, I think it's time for me to go home. I need to figure out what God wants me to do next."

June studied her face then nodded slowly. "I'll pray for you," she said.

"Excuse us!" Two muscular men rolled a heavy folding table past them. With a loud bang, they set it into place. Celie tied a tulle bow and cut the extra ribbon. When she was finished, all the trees lining the runway would have bows. Tomorrow she'd place tin buckets filled with freshly harvested apples along the path the models would walk.

"Have you told Matthew?"

"No, but I will."

"Celie! Am I doing this right?" Jill Lane, who was wearing blue pants with a stripe down the side, had obviously just gotten off her shift at the police department.

"Perfect!" Celie applauded as Jill strutted past them, lifting her knees high and keeping her gaze fixed on the treetops.

"When?" June pressed.

"Today, I promise. Mr. Beecham, please move that table a little more to the left." The sudden blare of music from the loudspeakers nearly made her drop the roll of tulle. She recovered just in time to watch Mrs. Innetti walk past, beaming and waving regally to an imaginary audience.

"You're doing great." Celie smiled as the tall brunette walked past. "You're right in step with the music."

"Stop waving your hands and start moving your hips more," June ordered. "This is a fashion show, not a royal wedding."

Another table rolled into view, followed by a group of women carrying folding chairs. Celie recognized Betty Rogers, Amanda Jackson, and Leslie Yazmine from the church choir. Behind them, pulling a dolly loaded high with chairs, was Matthew.

He wore a simple blue T-shirt and a light wash pair of jeans. Just ordinary clothing but so exactly right for him; she couldn't imagine him in anything else. Her breathing grew quicker as he neared.

"The ladies are done setting up the tables in the driveway for the rummage sale," he said, wiping the sweat from his face with the shoulder of his shirt. "They want to know if they should put the signs up tonight or wait until they put the clothing out tomorrow morning."

June turned to Celie. "I think tomorrow would be fine, don't you?"

Celie nodded. She didn't really want to think about the clothing neatly folded into boxes. She had to tell him about her leaving, but she didn't want to.

"Okay, I'll tell them." He looked at Celie. She remained frozen and mute.

June said, "Excuse me, but I want to make sure the sound crew has the right music."

Alone, Celie looked up into Matthew's beautiful face. A

wave of confusion passed through her. "Um," she said.

"Um?" He smiled, and for a moment everything felt like it was going to be okay. But was leaving really the right thing?

"Um." She paused, bit her lip, and steeled her resolve. "I wanted you to know I'm leaving. I'm going back to Ohio." There, she'd said it. She searched his eyes to read his reaction.

"You're leaving?" His lips tightened. "When?"

"Tomorrow. After the fashion show."

"Oh," he said. Was it her imagination, or did he relax slightly? Her shoulders slumped at the thought.

"You have my cell phone number. Will you call me when you hear from Kiera?"

"Of course."

That was it? He wasn't even going to try and stop her? "Thank you, Matthew, for letting me stay here." Her throat grew tight. "You and your mother have been so good to me."

"Look," Matthew continued, and she knew a moment's hope when he looked into her eyes. "I know we got off to a rough start—I was pretty hard on you. I. . ." For the first time, he seemed to struggle to find the right words. "I blamed you for introducing Kiera to the wrong crowd. I thought you'd supported a destructive relationship." He paused, wiped his face, and continued. "I was wrong, though. I just wanted you to know that."

Celie could only nod. Her throat was too tight to talk. The loudspeaker blared out the opening notes to "The Star Spangled Banner," and June's voice shouted, "No, no, no! That's wrong."

The music was a minor wrong compared to the greater sense of wrongness in Celie's heart as she watched Matthew tip back the dolly and walk away from her.

twenty-seven

Celie woke to a picture-perfect August day. The sun shone brightly, and the sky was a perfect shade of cerulean blue. Even the temperature cooperated, hovering in the low eighties.

She spent the morning helping the caterers place crisp white tablecloths on the tables and fill glass vases with wildflowers picked from the pastures on Jeremy's land. Lilac Westover and Esther Polino arrived and helped line the runway with tin buckets piled high with shiny Early Macs—the first of the orchard's harvest—and wind the backs of the folding chairs with yet more tulle.

Before Celie knew it, it was time to get the models ready. Within moments, Celie had her hands full. Barbara Willis zapped herself in the eye with a can of hair spray, Mrs. Innetti couldn't zip her dress, and Shirley Elliot stumbled in her stilettos, knocking off her glasses, which Jill Lane accidentally stepped on and broke. If this wasn't enough, Esther Polino had gotten a case of stage fright so bad that she had locked herself in the bathroom.

"Come on out, Esther," Celie coaxed the librarian from the other side of the door.

"I can't do it," Esther moaned. "Sorry, Celie."

"You can do it," Celie said, trying to sound calm when her own nerves jangled.

"Can't," Esther moaned. "My stomach feels awful." She paused. "I think I might throw up."

Celie remembered how she felt after eating an entire pie in less than five minutes. "Keep swallowing," she encouraged. "You have a little stage fright, that's all."

"Celie!" Shirley Elliot called. "We have a problem. I can't

see without my glasses!"

Something crashed in the kitchen—it sounded like a stack of plates—and then someone yelled, "Oh my stars!"

Celie ran into the kitchen to see what was going on and stopped in her tracks when she saw Kiera crouched on the floor helping the caterer pick up pieces of broken china.

Laughing, Kiera said, "This is so totally my fault, Gina. I am such a klutz. Always have been and always will be," she added cheerfully.

"Kiera?"

Kiera's blue eyes lit up when she saw Celie standing there, and she jumped to her feet and opened her arms.

With a happy cry, Celie launched herself forward and hugged her friend as hard as she could. "I can't believe you're here!"

"Celie, I can't breathe."

"Sorry." Celie released her grip and stepped back to examine her friend. "You look great. You're so tan. I'm so happy to see you! When did you get back?"

"Last night." Kiera tucked a strand of blond hair behind her ear. Her silver hoop earrings flashed almost as brightly as the big smile she gave Celie. "Hold on. First things first. I want you to meet Benji." She motioned to a bald, middle-aged man of medium height standing just inside the back door. A Nikon with a huge lens hung from his neck. "Benji, this is Celie Donovan—one of my best friends in the world. Celie, this is my husband, Benjamin Batemen—the love of my life."

Celie blinked. Husband? Kiera was married? And to this man? In the past, Kiera had gone either for male models or rich, powerful men. In his floral shirt and Bermuda shorts, Benji radiated neither power nor wealth. He did, however, have a friendly smile and a firm handshake.

"Celie, dear," June said, walking into the kitchen. "Lilac isn't sure whether to wear hoops or pendant earrings. Could you. . ." The rest of her sentence died on her lips. She moved faster than Celie had seen her move since she'd arrived and wrapped Kiera in her arms. They were of identical height and build. Even their hair color was only shades apart.

Celie sighed with pleasure. They both looked so happy. She heard a soft click and turned to see Benji lowering his camera. He gave her an apologetic smile. "She likes my pictures."

When at last June released Kiera, the older woman's face was flushed and tears streamed down her face. She held Kiera at arm's length, studying every inch of her and visibly trembling. "Oh thank God," June said. "Thank God you're home."

"Of course I'm home," Kiera said, wiping her own flushed face. "Mom," she said shyly. "Benji and I got married. The ship's captain did the ceremony on our way home."

"Married?" June's gaze swung between her daughter and her new son-in-law. "Married?"

"I love him," Kiera said simply.

The back door creaked open. "They're almost ready for dessert," Jeremy Taylor reported, slightly out of breath, as if he'd run all the way from the grandfather orchard to tell them. "Matthew says fifteen minutes until showtime."

Celie's heart skipped a beat. Esther Polino was still bolted inside the bathroom, and Shirley Elliot needed another pair of glasses.

"What do you want me to do?" Kiera asked. "How can I help?"

Kiera was a professional model. The best way to have her help was to put her in the show.

"There's a green dress upstairs in your closet," June said, following the direction of Celie's thoughts as if she had spoken them aloud, "wrapped in a plastic dry cleaning bag. Put it on, dear, and come get in line. You'll close out the show."

"We haven't done a fitting," Celie said.

June smiled at her. Her face glowed. In less than five

minutes, she seemed to have taken ten years off her age. "I have a feeling it will fit Kiera perfectly."

ଛ

Celie heard the music as she walked out the back door. Behind her, the models, each wearing one of her redesigns, fell into step as they crossed the grassy backyard and stepped into the mottled light of the orchards.

Her heart pounded in her chest, and her mouth went dry at the sight of the round tables with their crisp white table-cloths, wildflower arrangements, and gleaming white china. She could hardly bring herself to look at the townspeople filling every seat, turning to watch as she and the models neared.

Celie lifted her chin a notch and forced a confident smile. Esther Polino had had the right idea. The two of them should have stayed in the restroom. Her stomach rolled. Dear God, she simply wasn't cut out for this. If she didn't throw up, it'd be a miracle.

Matthew stood at the start of the runway, wearing a dark gray suit that had to be much too warm for the hot summer day. He had his arms folded and feet planted solidly over the grass he'd been cutting just the night before. Only a small nick on his chin where he'd cut himself shaving that morning suggested any hint of nerves. He was smiling, but the expression didn't quite reach his eyes.

The murmur of voices hushed. Celie glanced over her shoulder at the nervous but excited expressions on the women behind her, then she nodded at Matthew, who gave the signal. The music changed, and Celie gently urged Jill Lane forward.

The slender policewoman was wearing one of the first outfits Celie had created—a black pencil skirt and a patterned gray and olive blouse that in its last life had been a T-shirt. She'd tied a hand-knit gold scarf around Jill's neck. A pair of black boots—Celie's Jimmy Choos—finished off the outfit. Jill had her hands on her hips and swaggered down the grassy aisle with all the attitude of a Paris runway model. Celie could not have been prouder. Jill hit a pose at the end of the runway, and Benji fired off at least ten shots. People began applauding.

Mrs. Innetti went next in the yellow sundress outfit. She tottered off a little unsteadily in high heels that put her over the six-foot mark, but she seemed to pick up speed as she went.

Then it was Sally Netherlands's turn in the patterned scarf that had been turned into a wrap skirt, then Shirley Elliot who walked a perfectly straight line despite her lack of glasses, then Esther Polino who showed not one trace of nerves as she pranced down the runway in the tiered ruffle dress.

Click! Click! Click! More applause. More models marched down the runway, backs straight and chins held high. Lilac Westover received enthusiastic applause when she trotted out in the modified tuxedo.

Emily Taylor went next in a short black cocktail dress. With her long hair swept into an updo and the dress hugging her curves, she looked more beautiful than Celie had ever seen her. The audience seemed to think so, too. There were oohs and aahs, and somebody whistled. It wasn't Matthew— Celie was standing right next to him—but she didn't let herself look at his face, either.

And then it was Kiera's turn.

Celie caught her breath at the sight of her friend. The dress looked as if someone had poured a bucket of green silk over her head and the fabric had magically molded itself to Kiera's slender body.

A hush fell over the crowd as Kiera stepped out, every inch of her five-foot-ten frame working. Before she'd reached the first table, everyone was standing, applauding. The noise only grew louder as Kiera prowled down the runway, seeming to see no one and to walk with a confidence that suggested she owned the runway. At the end of the runway, she struck a pose as Benji snapped off shot after shot.

Suddenly Celie didn't care that no one else would ever see this dress. All that mattered was that it represented everything good that had happened to her here at the orchards. Kiera stepped forward, the dress flowing around her long, slender legs. Celie remembered the breeze on her cheeks when she and Matthew had taken a carriage ride around the orchards. She hadn't realized it when she'd been sewing the dress, but she knew now every stitch had been sewn with love. Love of these orchards. Of June. Of Matthew.

Kiera beamed at Celie as she stepped off the runway, signaling the end to the fashion show. Now Celie, as designer, would lead the models for one final turn down the runway. Celie's feet seemed suddenly rooted to the spot, and her Jell-O knees were wobbling.

Jill nudged Celie's arm. "They're waiting."

"I know."

Matthew glanced down at her. His blue eyes crinkled at the corners. "You're getting a standing ovation, but you'd better get out there."

She looked down the long lane between the trees, saw people clapping, smiling. June and Jeremy stood shoulder to shoulder, applauding and motioning for her to come forward. She hesitated, understanding finally that it wasn't stage fright that kept her rooted to the spot. She simply didn't want the fashion show to end. She didn't want to go back to Centerville, either.

"I don't want to go," she said.

"It's just stage fright." Matthew smiled in encouragement. "You can do it. They all loved your fashions."

She shook her head. "I mean I don't want to go—as in go back to Ohio." He still didn't seem to get it. She bunched her hands into fists and looked straight up at him. "Helping your mom with a canning business sounds pretty good."

He laughed. For a moment something very intense flashed in his blue eyes, and her heart did a long, slow turn in her chest. He wanted her to stay. She was sure of it. But then his jaw tightened in determination, and he shook his head. "You need to go. You need to get out there now," he clarified, pulling her forward.

She had a choice: walk with him willingly or risk being dragged across the grass. Celie lifted her chin and walked with him onto the runway. Forcing a smile to her stiff lips, she waved at the blur of faces in front of her.

Plain as day, she'd practically told him she loved him— right in front of who knew how many people—and the best he could do was say, *You need to go?* And then the not-so-romantic way he'd tugged her arm to get her moving.

Celie wanted to jerk away from Matthew, but he kept his fingers firmly wrapped around her hand. Wasn't he afraid that Emily Taylor would see him holding Celie's hand? Matthew would never have told Emily Taylor, *You need to get out there.*

An excited bark broke her thoughts. Ahead, Celie spotted Toaster, looking like a pirate king in a purple satin jacket with grommet closures. The small dog strained at his leash as Celie neared. June had the leash firmly wrapped around one hand. The other hand was holding onto Jeremy Taylor's hand. Celie swallowed a lump at the loving look June gave her.

It helped steady her and allowed her, moments later, to give James a genuine smile when she saw him.

James had his arm around his wife, Frieda, who was beautiful in a pale yellow silk shirt and patterned skirt—the very outfit Celie had designed for her birthday last May. And then her breath caught as she saw the tall, silver-haired man in gray Armani standing beside James. Her footsteps faltered, and she clutched Matthew's arm. "Matthew, it's him. It's George Marcus—my old boss."

Matthew glanced down at her. He had a pinched look about his mouth, and his eyes didn't quite hold her gaze. "I know."

"What's he doing here?"

"Right now he's applauding."

It was true. George Marcus was giving his signature three-beat clap. Celie's heart raced. How was this possible? Her gaze shot to James, beaming at her, and then back to George Marcus, who met her gaze and gave her a short, curt but unmistakable nod of approval.

"Breathe, Celie."

She gripped Matthew's hand more tightly and forced herself to exhale. The rest of the runway passed in a blur. She barely registered Benji taking shot after shot, and somehow she reached the beginning of the runway again. Everyone swarmed around them. Matthew stepped back as people rushed to congratulate her.

twenty-eight

The shears whispered through the fine threads of the black silk fabric as Celie concentrated on cutting the exact line of the pattern. At this phase, the dress looked like abstract art, a smattering of geometric shapes that shared nothing more in common than the fabric on which they lay. She freed a crescent-shaped piece that would become part of a bodice and laid it aside.

Straightening, she swept her bangs behind her ear. They'd grown long enough to stay there now, and she absently considered getting a new cut. She could afford it now. And get her nails done. While she was at it, she'd get a pedicure to go with the new Jimmy Choo peep-toe pumps. She was a full-fledged designer now. She still couldn't believe Libby Ellman was gone. The head designer had resigned. "To avoid being fired," George Marcus had explained after the Castoffs to Couture show had ended. "Our house does not steal designs," he explained and then smiling, had added, "We hire the designers who create the dresses we wish we had designed in the first place. Will you work for me?"

Celie freed a panel of the skirt next and put it aside. The job offer had been everything she'd wanted, and yet she wasn't nearly as happy to be back as she thought she'd be.

"Hey," a familiar voice said, and James popped into view. "Heard you're making a dress for Grace Bradley. You going to help her anchor the evening news, too?"

Celie set the scissors down. "Absolutely," she joked. "She'll interview people, and then I'll critique their clothing." James was balancing a large cheese Danish and two Styrofoam cups on a cardboard tray.

James set the tray down on another cutting table. "The

Danish is for you. I told Frieda you've lost ten pounds since you've been back. She told me to invite you home this weekend. She'll make you fettuccine Alfredo." He handed her one of the cups. "Say good-bye to your cholesterol," he added cheerfully.

June liked to fatten up people—and animals, too, Celie thought with a pang.

She picked an edge off the Danish and nibbled it more for James's sake than out of hunger. "That's nice of her. I'm fine, though."

James made a scoffing noise. "You're not fine. You've got huge bags under your eyes, and you're white as a sheet. What time did you leave last night? Did you even leave?"

It was Lipton tea, and James had added a generous amount of sugar. She sipped it gratefully, welcoming its warmth. "Of course I left." She didn't tell him that she'd taken the last train out of Grand Central or that the bags under her eyes had nothing to do with working too hard. She just couldn't seem to sleep anymore. She'd toss and turn and end up at the small window in the bedroom, remembering another view in another house.

"It's Matthew, isn't it?" His voice gentled. "You really miss him, don't you?"

Celie stuck the lid back on her tea. "What are you talking about, James? This job was what I always wanted. This spring I'm going to Paris!" She remembered just in time to smile.

James wasn't fooled. "You should call him."

Call him after the way she'd practically thrown herself at him? She stood. "Thanks for your concern, James, but I really don't want to talk about it."

"Like I couldn't figure *that* out." James sipped his coffee placidly. "You practically bite my head off every time I bring up his name." He held his hand up as she started to protest. "Look, you're like a daughter to me—the daughter me and Frieda never had." He paused. "All I want is for you to be happy. Matthew said that you belonged here. I thought you did, too, but now I'm realizing that we both got it wrong."

Celie, who had started to move away, froze in her tracks. "What do you mean Matthew said I belonged here?"

James turned his cup slowly in his hands. "All he wanted, Celie, was to give you the choice."

"What are you talking about?"

"To get your old job back. We discussed it when he came here."

"He came here? Matthew?"

"Three times," James confirmed. "He sat in the lobby trying to get George Marcus to see him. Just sat there, holding your dress. Wouldn't leave until George saw him personally."

Celie searched James's eyes. "He did?"

"Absolutely. Nadine was supposed to call security, but she didn't. She kept telling Libby that someone was on the way." He grinned. "She always thought it was wrong the way Libby fired you."

"She shouldn't have done that. She could have lost her job!"

"Word kind of spread, Celie, what Matthew was doing. All your friends here conspired to get him into George's office. It took us two days, but we finally figured it out. Connie from maintenance pretended to be this rich buyer from Madrid and kept Libby on the telephone. Surhina intercepted George's two o'clock appointment and flirted with him in the conference room. You need to know, Celie, Milah came forward, as well, and told George how you covered for her singeing a dress." His eyes looked sad. "You should have told me what really happened."

Celie sank back onto the stool and put her head in her hands. June had offered to hang the green silk in her closet because it had more room. Now she realized she must have been helping Matthew. "I. . .I don't know what to say. I didn't know. You all did that for me?"

"Of course we did." James patted her shoulder. "You think Connie's forgotten the wedding dress you made for her daughter? Or who took the blame when Surhina broke

Libby's sewing machine? Who went to court with Nadine over child support issues?"

Celie lifted her gaze. "Why didn't you tell me about this before?"

"Matthew asked me not to tell you. He thought it was better that way."

Matthew's face flashed through her mind. She felt the familiar pain and longing. She remembered standing with Matthew on the back porch the night after the fashion show. June had gone to bed, and they had discussed George's offer. He'd said, "If you don't take this job, Celie, you'll always wonder what you could have done."

She pushed Matthew's image away. "He just wanted to get rid of me."

"Celie." James's voice rang more sharply than she had ever heard it. "Are you blind as a bat? A man who spends three days sitting in the lobby even after Libby Ellman threatened to have him arrested—not to mention highly insulted his suit—was trying to get rid of you?" He raked his hand through his thin dark gray hair. "The only time that man looked beat was *after* George Marcus saw your dress and said he loved it."

Celie stood, sat down, then stood again. She paced the floor, pausing to look at James who apparently wasn't angry at her anymore. By the half smile on his face, he seemed fairly satisfied that he'd sent her emotions into a tailspin.

He wanted her to take the job but not because he wanted to get rid of her. Because it was what he thought she wanted more than anything.

She glanced at the clock, mentally calculating how long it would take her to get home, pack some clothes, and get her Honda.

Too long, she decided. She'd skip packing and simply drive. If she didn't hit traffic, she could be there by eight o'clock.

twenty-nine

Matthew was in his office working on invoices when the front doorbell rang. Toaster, who'd been sleeping in his lap, sprinted for the front door, barking his head off.

He frowned and pushed back his desk chair. Too late for a social call, he walked quickly to the door. June and Jeremy were on the road tonight—dinner and a movie. It was a beautiful October night, but accidents happened. The irony of him worrying about June being out on a date would have made him smile if he wasn't so worried.

The sight of Celie standing in the doorway hit him just like a punch to the stomach. He could only stand there, looking at her, aching to take her in his arms. He forced himself to stand so still it felt as if his body had turned to stone.

Toaster shot through the opening and jumped up on Celie's knees, shamelessly begging for her attention.

Matthew gripped the brass doorknob so tightly he thought he would crush it. "Hello, Celie."

"Matthew."

She looked thinner than he remembered—her collarbone more prominent—and there were purple shadows beneath her eyes. He pulled the door wider. "Come in."

She passed him on a pair of high-heeled shoes. Her perfume, the faintest hint of something floral, drifted past him as she crossed into the foyer. His heart beat hard at the sight of her once again in the house.

"June's out with Jeremy. A date." Matthew wondered if he had lost the power to speak a complete sentence. He tried again. "Can I get you something to eat or drink?"

Her smile seemed a little tight. "No thanks."

He frowned at the dog. "Toaster, will you stop? She already greeted you."

"It's okay, Matthew. I'm glad to see him, too."

"You want to sit in the living room while you wait for June?" Matthew folded his arms in what he hoped was a casual pose.

"Actually," Celie said, "I'm not here to see June."

"Well, Kiera's in Storrs, meeting Benji's family. Turns out the Batemans raise dairy cows. I don't think either Kiera or Benji has a farming bone in their body. They both want to live in New York City." He was rambling but couldn't seem to help himself.

"I know," Celie said. "I didn't come to see Kiera, either." She paused, her eyes dark and luminous as she looked up at him. "I came to see you, Matthew."

The October night was cool, but he felt himself start to perspire. He tried to swallow, but his throat was inexplicably parched. "Why?"

"James told me you were the one who convinced George Marcus to look at my dress—and give me my old job back." Celie pushed a strand of shiny hair behind her ear. He noticed it did not fall forward again. She shifted her weight, and it occurred to him she might be as nervous as he was.

"I...um...wanted to thank you for doing that."

He didn't want her thanks or for her visit to be motivated by gratitude. "You're welcome." Disappointment weighed over him, but he forced a smile to his lips. "You didn't have to come all this way to tell me that."

"I know. But I want to know why. Why would you do that, Matthew? Why would you go into New York City—a place you hate?"

Matthew shifted his weight. "I don't hate Manhattan. And I didn't want to let them get away with stealing your design. I figured if George Marcus saw your original, which I knew had to be better, he'd do the right thing, if he were honest. And if he wasn't honest, he had to know we were going to fight him legally."

"You'd do that for me?"

"Of course."

Go ahead and tell her, something deep inside him insisted. *Tell her how you really feel.* His feet seemed to step forward of their own accord.

He stood within an arm's reach now, and all at once a deep calm came over him, as if all his questions had been asked and answered. The fears and doubts were replaced with a quiet certainty.

"Celie, I wanted to give you what you wanted, what you deserve, because. . .I love you." He looked deeply into her eyes. "I'm in love with you."

Celie's cheeks turned red. Her eyes shone as she looked up at him.

"I'm in love with you," Matthew repeated. "It almost killed me to let you go once. I promised myself if you came back I'd tell you how I felt." His heart thudded so loudly he wondered if he could even hear her response.

"I love you, too, Matthew."

He reached for her hands. To hear her say she loved him filled him with a joy beyond his wildest dreams. "I've loved you," he said, "from the moment you outran Happy the goat."

"I'm never going to live that down, am I?" Celie replied, but her eyes sparkled. She squeezed his hands. "I don't know when I started loving you, Matthew. It just took me awhile to figure it out." She shook her head ruefully. "We can thank Emily Taylor for part of that."

Matthew shook his head. "You were jealous?" He felt a rush of pleasure then the need to reassure her. "It's you, Celie, I want. Just you." The words seemed to release the last bit of weight that had been on his shoulders since the day of the fashion show. He got down on one knee. "You won't live an exciting life here, Celie, but it'll be a happy one. As happy as I can make it. Will you marry me?"

Her eyes went wide with shock, then a deep glow of

happiness seemed to radiate from her. "I would be proud to be your wife. Yes, Matthew, I'll marry you."

"You won't have to give up your career. If you want to live in the city, we'll find a way to make that work. And if you want to stay here, I'll build you a sewing room on the back of the house. Whatever you want, Celie. I mean that."

"I want you," Celie said. "Now and forever. I want to grow old with you. I want to see you sitting under that quilt with our kids. Teaching them to be the kind of person you are."

Matthew didn't think he deserved that kind of praise, but he was determined to spend the rest of his life trying to live up to it. With God's help, maybe he could. He thought his heart would explode with joy when he put his arms around her. Such a tiny woman, and yet she fit so perfectly against him. He could feel her heart beating, a strong and steady pulse against his chest.

He'd always thought home was this orchard, this land where two generations of his family had lived. Looking down into Celie's beautiful brown eyes, he realized there was a whole other kind of belonging.

epilogue

A year and a half later

"Hold still, Celie. Your veil is slipping." Linda Donovan's hands were cold but steady as she adjusted the lace. "There." She smiled tearfully into her daughter's face. "I love you so much."

"I'm so glad you're here." Celie blinked back her own tears as she wrapped her mother into another hug. "I love you, too."

Click. Click. Click. Celie lost count as Benji Bateman fired off another round of photographic shots in rapid succession. She could feel her mother's heart pounding beneath the taffeta folds of her navy dress. "I'm so happy for you," her mother whispered. "To find love is such a blessing."

"You sure you aren't disappointed about me not working in Manhattan?" Celie hadn't meant the question to slip out, but now that it had, she couldn't simply will it back.

Her mother shook her head. "All I've ever wanted was for you to be happy. Didn't you know that?"

"But you've made so many sacrifices."

"You're special, Celie. I wanted the world to see that. But as far as what you do with your gifts, that's up to you and God. I'll be proud of you no matter what."

"Keep talking," Benji instructed, clicking away. "Pretend I'm not here. Can you move a little to your left, Celie?"

Celie sighed and did as he asked.

"You're going to thank him after you see the photos." Kiera adjusted one of the backlights. "I didn't remember half of what happened at my wedding until I saw the photos."

Benji and Kiera mirrored happy grins. "You two are a walking advertisement for marriage," Celie said.

"You'll see for yourself how wonderful marriage can be," Kiera promised. "I've never seen Matthew so excited and nervous in my entire life. He's checked the air pressure in the truck's tires at least twice."

"But we're flying to Paris for the honeymoon," Celie said.

Kiera laughed. "You have to drive to the airport first. He has three routes to Bradley planned in case of traffic. What can I say? The man's in love."

And so was she.

Someone knocked softly on the bedroom door, and June's smiling face appeared in the crack. "It's almost time. . . . Oh, Celie," she whispered reverently. "You're so beautiful."

"June!" Celie waved her inside. "Let me see you." June stepped into the room, her silk chiffon skirt rustling. Toaster's head peeked out from beneath the fullness of the skirt. Kiera grabbed him just before the small dog jumped up on Celie.

"Put the dog down," Celie said. "He's fine." She paused as she took in June's outfit. "You look amazing!" Celie clapped her hands together in delight.

"It should. You sewed it." June winked. "Toastie likes his pretty little lilac suit, too. Don't you, Toastie?" At the sound of his name, the dog trotted back to June. "But you, Celie,"—June put her hand on her heart—"are beautiful beyond words."

Benji fired off more shots as Celie hugged June. When she finally stepped back, she had to wipe the tears from her cheeks. "June. . .thank you so much for all you've done for me. For welcoming me into your home and into your family."

June's throat worked for a moment. "You, honey. We should be thanking you. You've brought a whole new light into our house and into our lives. I couldn't love you more if you were my own daughter. I thank God for the day you stepped into our lives."

Unshed tears turned Celie's world blurry. A happy kind of blurry, though.

"You're going to ruin your eye makeup, Celie, if you don't

stop crying," Kiera said. "Someone hand me a tissue please." She then proceeded to dry her own eyes. Celie couldn't help laughing, which was probably exactly what Kiera had intended.

"We'd better get going," June said. "We'll make Matthew a nervous wreck if we're late."

"Not just yet." Celie took Kiera's hand on one side and her mother's on the other. Her mother reached for June's hand, and soon everyone had formed almost a full circle. Everyone but Benji.

"Put your camera down," Kiera ordered her husband, who placidly continued photographing June's and Linda's joined hands.

"Someone has to record this," Benji protested. "Someone has to keep their emotions in check."

"We don't need a camera to remember this," June said, breaking her link to reach out to him. "We need you."

With the circle complete, Celie closed her eyes. "Heavenly Father," she said, "thank You for this beautiful day, for Matthew, June, Kiera, Benji, my parents, and everyone here today. I don't know what heaven will look like, but it's got to look a lot like this house and farm. Thank You, Father, for all the blessings you've sent us—especially the ones we don't always recognize as blessings."

When she finished, there was a big sniffle, and Benji said, "Would someone please hand me a Kleenex?"

It was a short walk to the spot in the grandfather grove—the very same spot where they'd had their fashion show. Neither her mom nor June had allowed her to see the decorations until now. The sight of the tulle bows and white gossamer ribbons hanging from the old trees almost took her breath away.

Matthew waited for her at the end of the aisle formed between the grandfather apple trees. He stood tall and very straight in a pin-striped charcoal gray suit that fit his frame perfectly. His face lit up when he saw her. The whole world seemed to fall away from her. All she wanted was waiting for her at the end of the tree-lined aisle.

She clutched her bouquet of gardenias and ordered herself not to cry. A gentle breeze touched her cheek, like a caress, and brought with it the faintest odor of apples. They were still on the trees, small clusters no larger than grapes, part of a cycle she was just beginning to understand.

The speakers crackled slightly, emitted a high-pitched ringing noise, then settled into the clear notes of the sonata she and Matthew had selected. People stood as Jeremy, resplendent in a light gray suit with a lavender bow, escorted June slowly down the grassy aisle. Toaster seemed to understand the importance of the occasion and walked solemnly at June's side with his head held high.

Her mother went next, then Celie was watching Kiera's back moving away from her. Kiera in the green silk dress— the one that relaunched both their careers and, even more importantly, helped bring her and Matthew back together.

The music paused, and the sound system gave another ominous crackle before starting the notes to Wagner's traditional march. Everyone stood. They were all there, everyone she loved, and she could see their faces shining with joy. Matthew waited for her, his arms at his side, his feet firmly planted on the close-cropped lawn. Matthew, who would stand strong with her no matter what problems came their way.

She suddenly couldn't wait to get down the aisle to be with him, to speak the vows that would bind them together. She linked her arm through her father's and smiled up into his familiar craggy profile. "Let's go."

He smiled, patted her fingers once, and then they stepped forward.

A Letter To Our Readers

Dear Reader:

In order that we might better contribute to your reading enjoyment, we would appreciate your taking a few minutes to respond to the following questions. We welcome your comments and read each form and letter we receive. When completed, please return to the following:

Fiction Editor
Heartsong Presents
PO Box 719
Uhrichsville, Ohio 44683

1. Did you enjoy reading *A Whole New Light* by Kim O'Brien?
   ☐ Very much! I would like to see more books by this author!
   ☐ Moderately. I would have enjoyed it more if

   _____

   _____

   _____

2. Are you a member of **Heartsong Presents**? ☐ Yes ☐ No
   If no, where did you purchase this book? _____

   _____

3. How would you rate, on a scale from 1 (poor) to 5 (superior), the cover design? _____

4. On a scale from 1 (poor) to 10 (superior), please rate the following elements.

   ____ Heroine   ____ Plot
   ____ Hero   ____ Inspirational theme
   ____ Setting   ____ Secondary characters

5. These characters were special because? _____

_____

_____

6. How has this book inspired your life? _____

_____

_____

7. What settings would you like to see covered in future
Heartsong Presents books? _____

_____

_____

8. What are some inspirational themes you would like to see
treated in future books? _____

_____

_____

9. Would you be interested in reading other **Heartsong
Presents** titles? ❑ Yes ❑ No

10. Please check your age range:

    ❑ Under 18   ❑ 18-24

    ❑ 25-34   ❑ 35-45

    ❑ 46-55   ❑ Over 55

Name _____

Occupation _____

Address _____

City, State, Zip _____

Heartsong

HEARTSONG PRESENTS TITLES AVAILABLE NOW:

Presents

Great Inspirational Romance at a Great Price!

Heartsong Presents books are inspirational romances in
contemporary and historical settings, designed to give you an
enjoyable, spirit-lifting reading experience. You can choose
wonderfully written titles from some of today's best authors like
Wanda E. Brunstetter, Mary Connealy, Susan Page Davis,
Cathy Marie Hake, Joyce Livingston, and many others.

When ordering quantities less than twelve, above titles are $2.97 each.
Not all titles may be available at time of order.